This book of monstrous stories
and rhymes belongs to

Craig F.

Monster Stories

First published in 2001 by Parragon

Parragon
Queen Street House
4 Queen Street
Bath BA1 1HE

Produced by
The Templar Company plc
Pippbrook Mill, London Road
Dorking, Surrey RH4 1JE

Designed by Caroline Reeves

Printed and bound in Italy

Hardback ISBN 0-75255-671-1
Paperback ISBN 0-75256-690-3

Monster Stories

Written by
Andy Charman, Beatrice Phillpotts, Caroline Repchuk,
Louisa Somerville and Christine Tagg

Illustrated by
Diana Catchpole, Robin Edmonds, Chris Forsey
and Claire Mumford

Contents

Monster Rap

"**B**UZZ BUZZ BUZZ,"
Went the Monster Fly.
"What's that I see
With my little eye?

It's a mean-looking plant,
But I'm sure I can cope.
The time has come
For it to give up hope.

My wings are HUGE,
I'm the size of a bike.
When you're big like me
You can do what you like!

The nectar's yummy,
The pollen's looking sweet,
This is gonna be
A real big treat.

I've got a big body
And fat hairy legs,
I'll suck up that plant
'Till the poor thing BEGS!"

Fat Fly buzzed in
And started to lick,
But that sneaky plant
Had one last trick.

SNAP! went the leaves,
CRUNCH! went the fly.
The last thing it heard
Was the plant laugh and sigh!

It's a trick!
It's a trap!
It's a Monster Fly Trap Rap!

Monster Marathon

"Very nice," said Cyril the Cyclops, eyeing his reflection in a puddle on the floor of his cave. He was wearing running shoes, running shorts, and a running vest. He practised some running on the spot but had to stop because his nose started running too. This was all part of his rigorous training programme, for Cyril the Cyclops had entered the annual Monster Marathon, and he had his eye on the trophy.

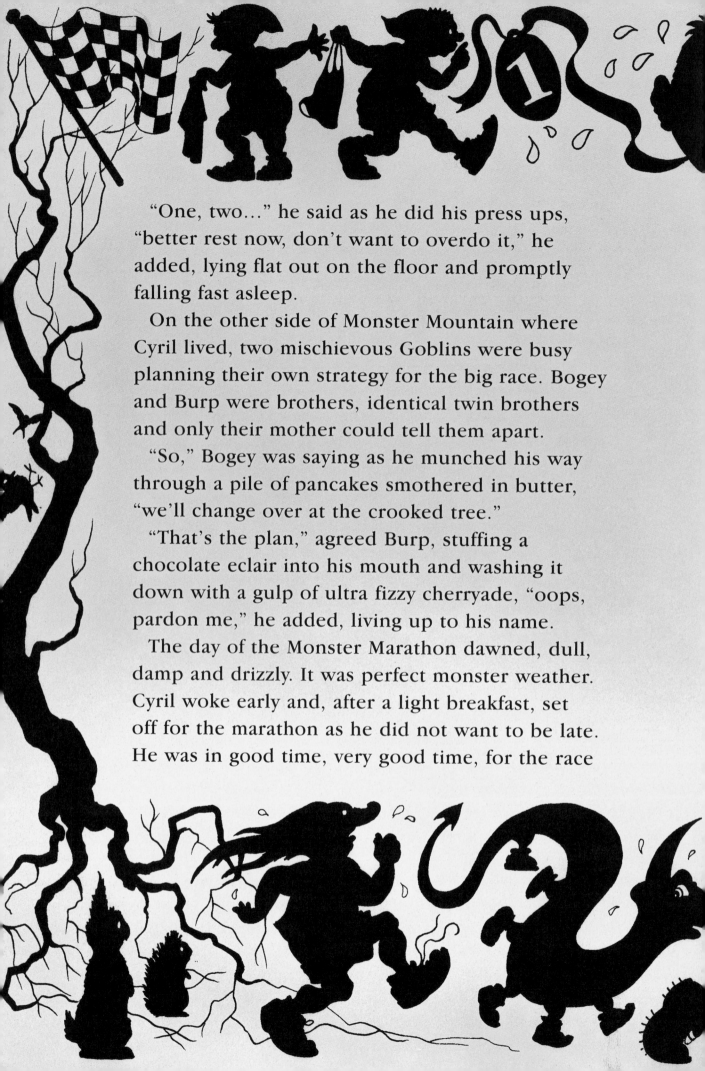

"One, two…" he said as he did his press ups, "better rest now, don't want to overdo it," he added, lying flat out on the floor and promptly falling fast asleep.

On the other side of Monster Mountain where Cyril lived, two mischievous Goblins were busy planning their own strategy for the big race. Bogey and Burp were brothers, identical twin brothers and only their mother could tell them apart.

"So," Bogey was saying as he munched his way through a pile of pancakes smothered in butter, "we'll change over at the crooked tree."

"That's the plan," agreed Burp, stuffing a chocolate eclair into his mouth and washing it down with a gulp of ultra fizzy cherryade, "oops, pardon me," he added, living up to his name.

The day of the Monster Marathon dawned, dull, damp and drizzly. It was perfect monster weather. Cyril woke early and, after a light breakfast, set off for the marathon as he did not want to be late. He was in good time, very good time, for the race

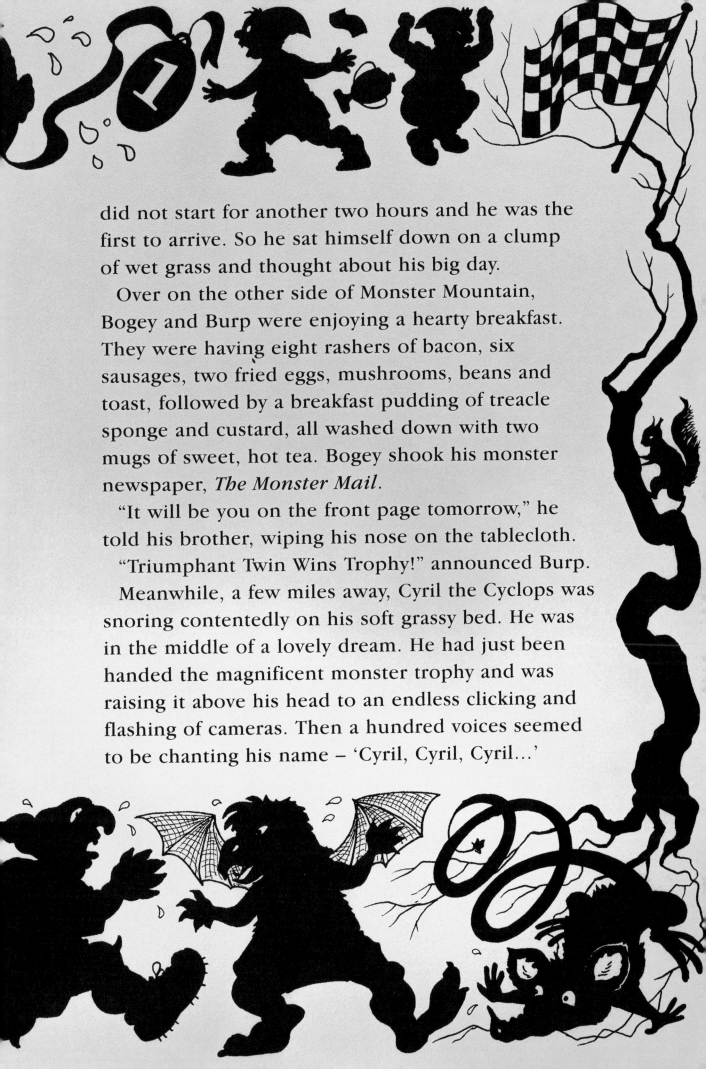

did not start for another two hours and he was the
first to arrive. So he sat himself down on a clump
of wet grass and thought about his big day.

Over on the other side of Monster Mountain,
Bogey and Burp were enjoying a hearty breakfast.
They were having eight rashers of bacon, six
sausages, two fried eggs, mushrooms, beans and
toast, followed by a breakfast pudding of treacle
sponge and custard, all washed down with two
mugs of sweet, hot tea. Bogey shook his monster
newspaper, *The Monster Mail*.

"It will be you on the front page tomorrow," he
told his brother, wiping his nose on the tablecloth.

"Triumphant Twin Wins Trophy!" announced Burp.

Meanwhile, a few miles away, Cyril the Cyclops was
snoring contentedly on his soft grassy bed. He was
in the middle of a lovely dream. He had just been
handed the magnificent monster trophy and was
raising it above his head to an endless clicking and
flashing of cameras. Then a hundred voices seemed
to be chanting his name – 'Cyril, Cyril, Cyril...'

"Cyril the Cyclops?" asked a short, stout, custard-coloured monster wearing a whistle around his neck and holding an important-looking clipboard. Cyril woke with a start and rubbed his eye.

"Yes, yes, that's me," confirmed Cyril as the stout monster ran his pencil down the list and ticked Cyril's name off. Cyril gazed around the field. Quite a lot had been going on whilst he had been asleep. Colourful flags fluttered in the breeze, a large banner that said 'ANNUAL MONSTER MARATHON' swung gently above his head, and the field itself was steadily filling up with all manner of monsters. Big monsters, little monsters, fat monsters and thin monsters. Cyril watched as a troop of trolls jogged by wearing matching tracksuits with *Team Troll* neatly embroidered on the back, looking very professional. He suddenly felt rather nervous.

The stout monster official was still wandering around the field with his clipboard and whistle, taking all the entrants' details as they arrived on the field.

"I only have one name down here," he explained as Bogey and Burp, the Goblin twins approached.

"That's correct," said Bogey. "My brother Burp here is running in the race and I am his coach." Bogey pointed to the scarlet tee shirt he was wearing which said 'Coach' on the front in large yellow letters. Burp burped "Oops, pardon, do excuse me," he said, wishing he hadn't had that second helping of treacle sponge.

"I see," said the monster official, gazing from one twin to the other and back again.

At long last the entrants were called to the starting line. Cyril nervously joined the crowd of runners. There must have been well over fifty. 'Oh dear,' he thought, feeling out of his depth. The monster official

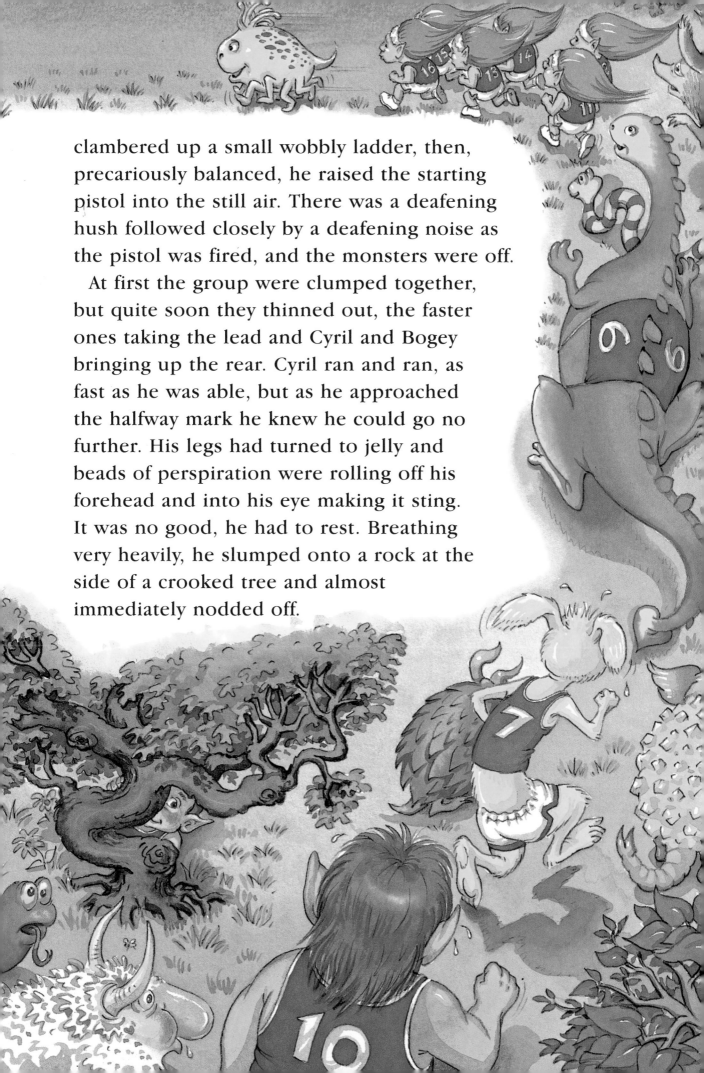

clambered up a small wobbly ladder, then, precariously balanced, he raised the starting pistol into the still air. There was a deafening hush followed closely by a deafening noise as the pistol was fired, and the monsters were off.

At first the group were clumped together, but quite soon they thinned out, the faster ones taking the lead and Cyril and Bogey bringing up the rear. Cyril ran and ran, as fast as he was able, but as he approached the halfway mark he knew he could go no further. His legs had turned to jelly and beads of perspiration were rolling off his forehead and into his eye making it sting. It was no good, he had to rest. Breathing very heavily, he slumped onto a rock at the side of a crooked tree and almost immediately nodded off.

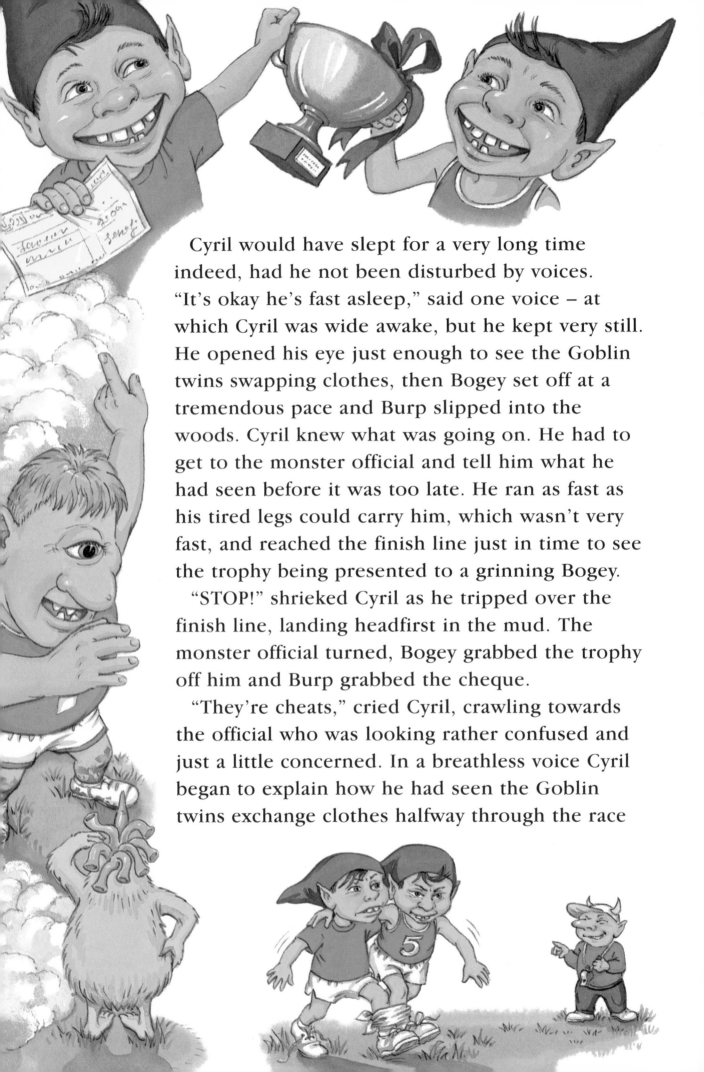

Cyril would have slept for a very long time indeed, had he not been disturbed by voices. "It's okay he's fast asleep," said one voice – at which Cyril was wide awake, but he kept very still. He opened his eye just enough to see the Goblin twins swapping clothes, then Bogey set off at a tremendous pace and Burp slipped into the woods. Cyril knew what was going on. He had to get to the monster official and tell him what he had seen before it was too late. He ran as fast as his tired legs could carry him, which wasn't very fast, and reached the finish line just in time to see the trophy being presented to a grinning Bogey.

"STOP!" shrieked Cyril as he tripped over the finish line, landing headfirst in the mud. The monster official turned, Bogey grabbed the trophy off him and Burp grabbed the cheque.

"They're cheats," cried Cyril, crawling towards the official who was looking rather confused and just a little concerned. In a breathless voice Cyril began to explain how he had seen the Goblin twins exchange clothes halfway through the race

and a fresh Bogey going on to complete the race.

"Nonsense," complained Burp, "I'm his coach, I trained him, my brother won fair and square." The monster official gazed suspiciously from one Goblin to the other then back again.

"Then why," he began slowly, pointing to Burp's tee shirt, "are your clothes on inside out?"

Cyril hadn't won the race of course, but he didn't mind because he was awarded an extra special medal for his vigilance and his sense of fair play. And as for the Goblin twins? Well, they didn't go home empty-handed either. The monster official arranged a special event just for them, a three legged race which they won without having to cheat at all, but only because no-one else bothered to enter. And they did make it on to the front page of *The Monster Mail*, too.

'**CYRIL SAVES THE DAY**', read the main headline the following morning, with a large picture of a smiling Cyril and underneath a much smaller headline which said simply, '**GOBLINS ARE A LAUGHING STOCK**'.

Maud and the Monster

Maud was quite a rascal,
A cheerful little tyke.
She used to say, "I do declare,
There's nothing I don't like!"

Slimy eggs and spiders' legs,
Nothing seemed to faze her.
She even liked the fuzzy bits,
That fell off Grandpa's razor.

One day, when Maud was feeling bored,
She passed the cellar door.
To her surprise, the light was on
And brave young Maud thought 'Cor!'

'I bet I could have loads of fun,
And fool around down there.'
And without a second thought,
She dashed straight down the stairs.

But when she reached the cellar floor,
She heard the door bang shut.
The light went off and, in the dark,
Maud really did her nut.

In the corner of the cellar
Stood a bright white monstrous shape.
This monster hummed a spooky tune,
Which made poor Maud go ape.

"Help me, save me!" Maud cried out.
"Call the coppers quick!
The monster's going to get me!
I'm so scared that I feel sick!"

The door burst open and in came Mum,
"You're afraid of that old geezer?"
Mum laughed. "If you look closely, Maud,
You'll see that it's the FREEZER!"

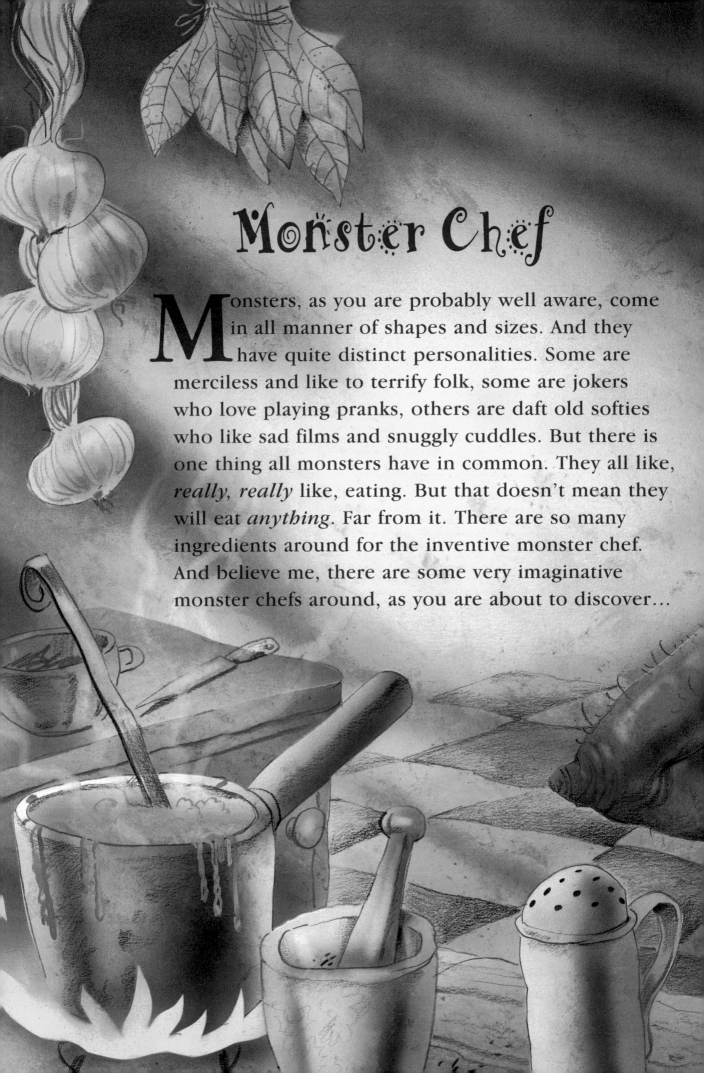

Monster Chef

Monsters, as you are probably well aware, come in all manner of shapes and sizes. And they have quite distinct personalities. Some are merciless and like to terrify folk, some are jokers who love playing pranks, others are daft old softies who like sad films and snuggly cuddles. But there is one thing all monsters have in common. They all like, *really, really* like, eating. But that doesn't mean they will eat *anything*. Far from it. There are so many ingredients around for the inventive monster chef. And believe me, there are some very imaginative monster chefs around, as you are about to discover…

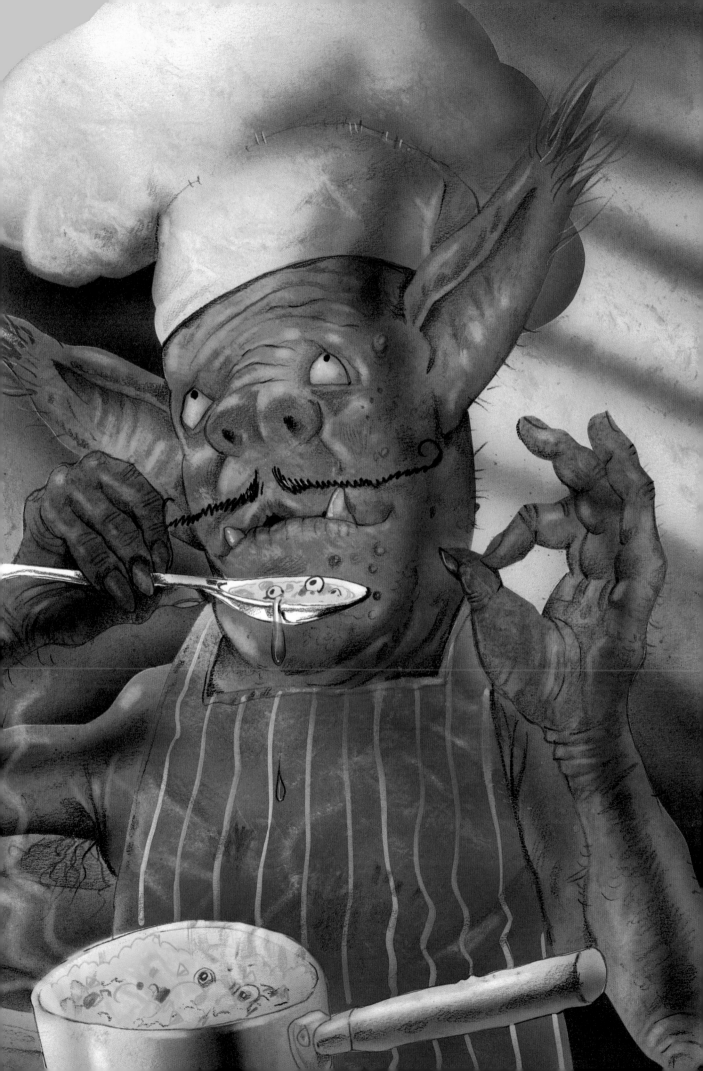

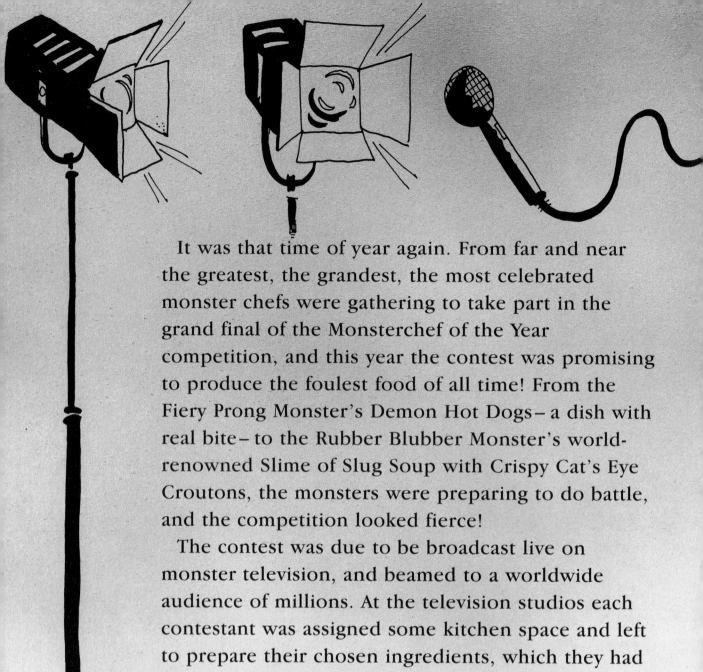

It was that time of year again. From far and near the greatest, the grandest, the most celebrated monster chefs were gathering to take part in the grand final of the Monsterchef of the Year competition, and this year the contest was promising to produce the foulest food of all time! From the Fiery Prong Monster's Demon Hot Dogs – a dish with real bite – to the Rubber Blubber Monster's world-renowned Slime of Slug Soup with Crispy Cat's Eye Croutons, the monsters were preparing to do battle, and the competition looked fierce!

The contest was due to be broadcast live on monster television, and beamed to a worldwide audience of millions. At the television studios each contestant was assigned some kitchen space and left to prepare their chosen ingredients, which they had brought with them in bags, buckets and cages!

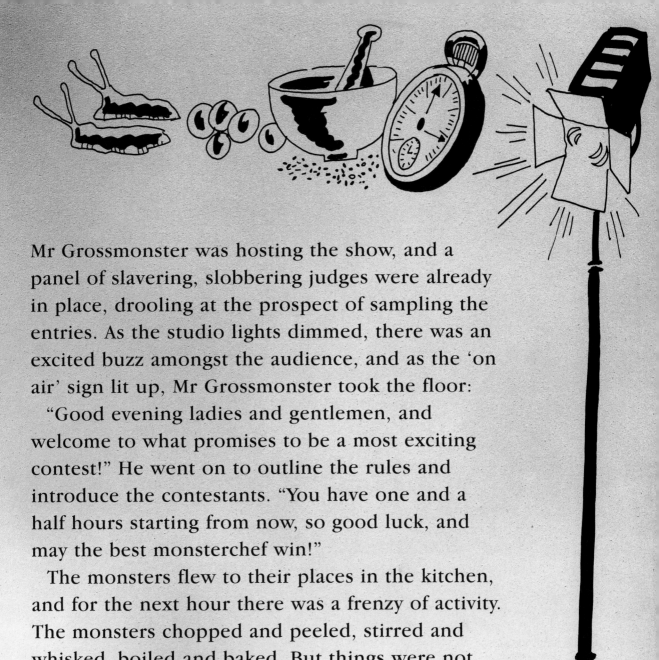

Mr Grossmonster was hosting the show, and a panel of slavering, slobbering judges were already in place, drooling at the prospect of sampling the entries. As the studio lights dimmed, there was an excited buzz amongst the audience, and as the 'on air' sign lit up, Mr Grossmonster took the floor:

"Good evening ladies and gentlemen, and welcome to what promises to be a most exciting contest!" He went on to outline the rules and introduce the contestants. "You have one and a half hours starting from now, so good luck, and may the best monsterchef win!"

The monsters flew to their places in the kitchen, and for the next hour there was a frenzy of activity. The monsters chopped and peeled, stirred and whisked, boiled and baked. But things were not going smoothly…

Far from it. The Hairy Scary Monster threw all his arms up in horror, as a simmering pot of stagnant sludge tipped and spilt all across the stove.

"My soup base!" he cried in despair. The Bug-eyed Monster's eyes boggled as the frogs' legs in his Frog Leg and Maggot Fricassee leapt out of the pan, and bounded in all directions, causing chaos around the studio. The Stinky Gas Monster screamed as his Oven Roast Rat and Bat Blood Casserole exploded just as Mr Grossmonster passed, spattering him from head to toe. And the Rancid Fat Monster howled as his frying pan burst into flames, burning his Pig Swill Pancakes to a crisp! And that was not all. Ovens mysteriously opened, deflating Pus and Scab Soufflés and Scary Fairy Cakes. Vats of giblets and gizzards boiled over. A Sweaty Sock Stew simply got up and hopped off.

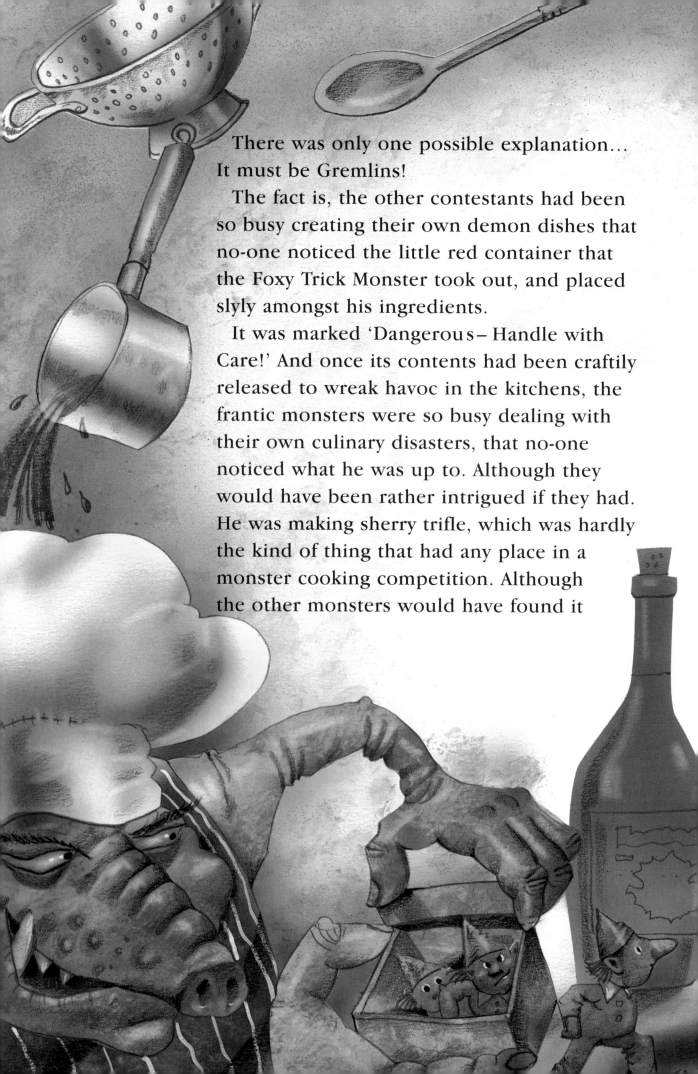

There was only one possible explanation…
It must be Gremlins!

The fact is, the other contestants had been
so busy creating their own demon dishes that
no-one noticed the little red container that
the Foxy Trick Monster took out, and placed
slyly amongst his ingredients.

It was marked 'Dangerous – Handle with
Care!' And once its contents had been craftily
released to wreak havoc in the kitchens, the
frantic monsters were so busy dealing with
their own culinary disasters, that no-one
noticed what he was up to. Although they
would have been rather intrigued if they had.
He was making sherry trifle, which was hardly
the kind of thing that had any place in a
monster cooking competition. Although
the other monsters would have found it

quite revolting, there was a certain type of monster that just loved it. Couldn't resist it. Couldn't get enough… Gremlins! So, once their mischievous mission was complete, the Foxy Trick Monster tempted them back to their box with generous helpings of sherry trifle, and then carried on cooking.

But time was ticking on, and the final countdown began. The distraught monsters struggled to salvage what they could from their kitchens as a frazzled Mr Grossmonster announced that their time was up. The panel of judges was called forward and the monsters presented the dismal remains of their dishes. The judges were so disgusted by the burnt offerings (not to mention disappointed at missing out on the tasting), that they disqualified each monster in turn.

All that is except for the Foxy Trick Monster.
When it came to his turn to present his dish, he
turned to the oven and took out a fine steaming
pie, with a thick golden crust, which looked…
perfect! The judges, the other monsters and the
studio audience gasped with astonishment!

They didn't even wait to taste it. Whatever was
in there could only be an improvement on the
other pathetic offerings. Without hesitation, the
judges came to a unanimous decision and
announced him the winner. "Well done!" said
poor flustered Mr Grossmonster, overcome
with relief at having someone to congratulate.

Without further ado, he handed the Foxy Trick
Monster the coveted silver cup at once.
The other monsters clapped politely,
and shook his hand.

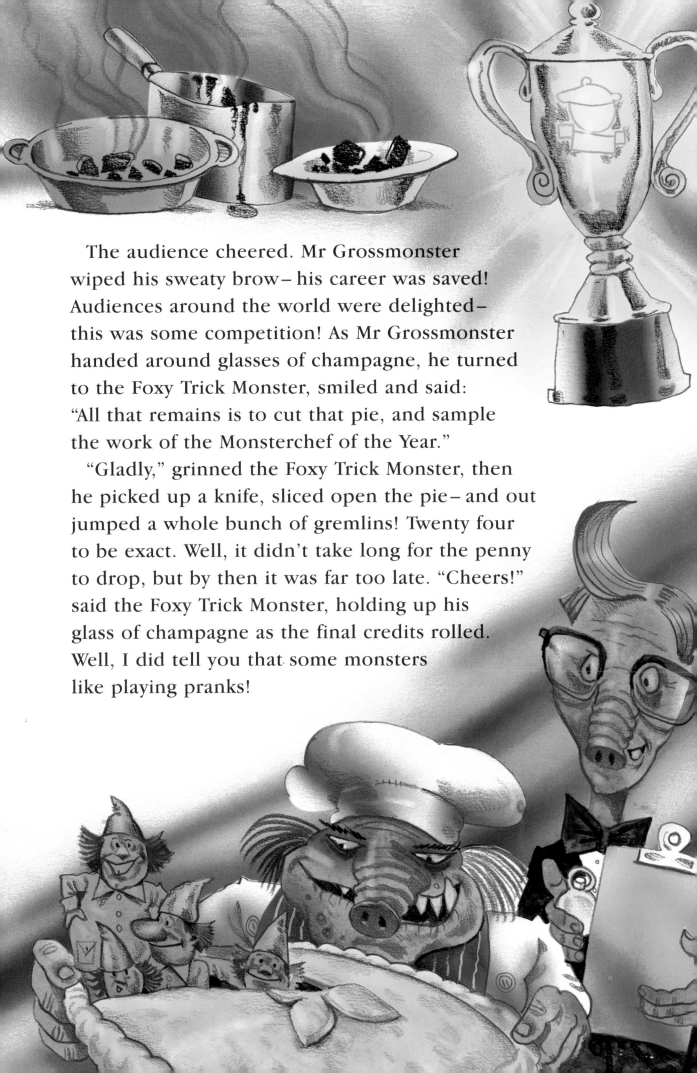

The audience cheered. Mr Grossmonster
wiped his sweaty brow – his career was saved!
Audiences around the world were delighted –
this was some competition! As Mr Grossmonster
handed around glasses of champagne, he turned
to the Foxy Trick Monster, smiled and said:
"All that remains is to cut that pie, and sample
the work of the Monsterchef of the Year."

"Gladly," grinned the Foxy Trick Monster, then
he picked up a knife, sliced open the pie – and out
jumped a whole bunch of gremlins! Twenty four
to be exact. Well, it didn't take long for the penny
to drop, but by then it was far too late. "Cheers!"
said the Foxy Trick Monster, holding up his
glass of champagne as the final credits rolled.
Well, I did tell you that some monsters
like playing pranks!

I'm the Deep Sea Monster

I'm the Deep Sea Monster,
I'm in a spot of trouble,
My joints are seizing up,
And I've started seeing double.

Getting hard of hearing,
(Or there's water in my ears),
Can't find my direction,
After many, many years!

All my teeth are rotting,
And my gums are getting slack,
My skin is full of wrinkles,
And a hump's grown on my back.

Guess I'll throw in the towel,
And I'll head for pastures new,
But please – would someone tell me,
What ex-Deep Sea Monsters do?

Troll Love

No-one in Fern's village had been able to go anywhere for months. They stayed in their shops and homes, or moped about on the green, waiting for something, or someone, to save them from the troll. The shepherds and the farmers kept their animals in the fields close to the centre. They didn't dare take them to the further pastures in case the troll attacked them and ate their animals.

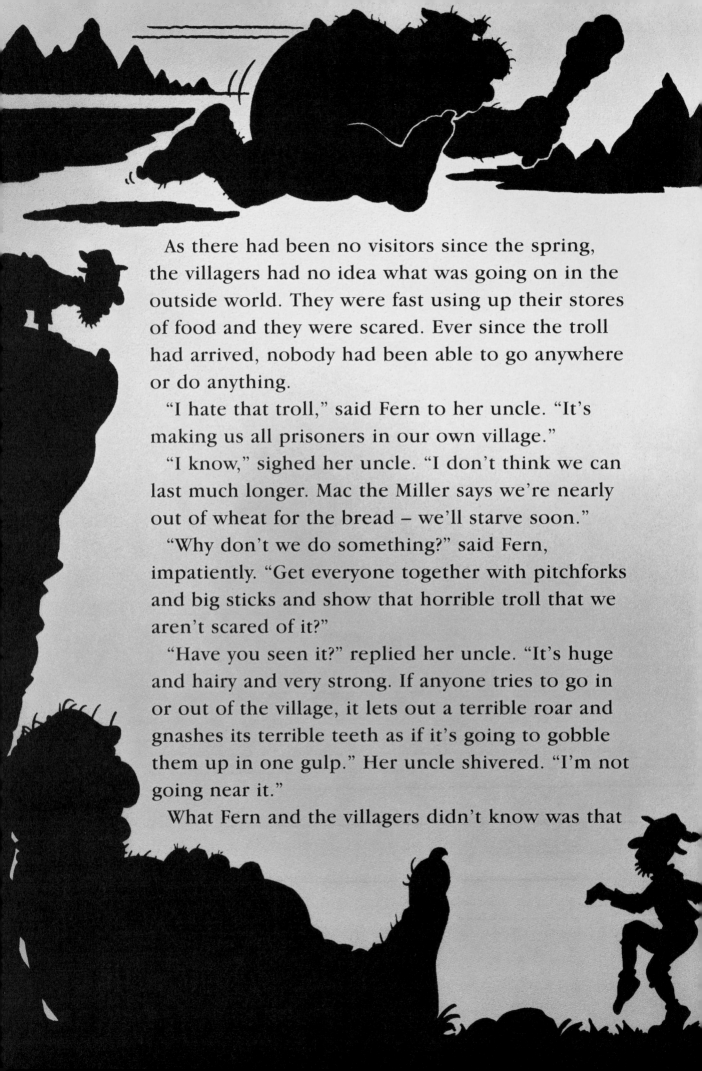

As there had been no visitors since the spring, the villagers had no idea what was going on in the outside world. They were fast using up their stores of food and they were scared. Ever since the troll had arrived, nobody had been able to go anywhere or do anything.

"I hate that troll," said Fern to her uncle. "It's making us all prisoners in our own village."

"I know," sighed her uncle. "I don't think we can last much longer. Mac the Miller says we're nearly out of wheat for the bread – we'll starve soon."

"Why don't we do something?" said Fern, impatiently. "Get everyone together with pitchforks and big sticks and show that horrible troll that we aren't scared of it?"

"Have you seen it?" replied her uncle. "It's huge and hairy and very strong. If anyone tries to go in or out of the village, it lets out a terrible roar and gnashes its terrible teeth as if it's going to gobble them up in one gulp." Her uncle shivered. "I'm not going near it."

What Fern and the villagers didn't know was that

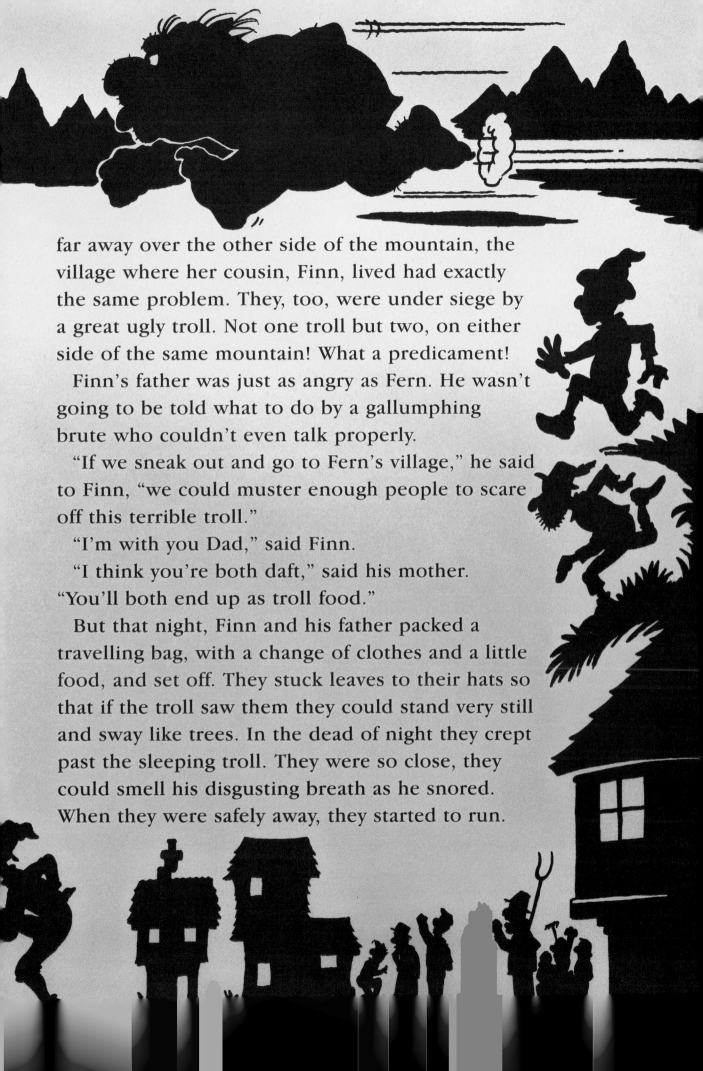

far away over the other side of the mountain, the village where her cousin, Finn, lived had exactly the same problem. They, too, were under siege by a great ugly troll. Not one troll but two, on either side of the same mountain! What a predicament!

Finn's father was just as angry as Fern. He wasn't going to be told what to do by a gallumphing brute who couldn't even talk properly.

"If we sneak out and go to Fern's village," he said to Finn, "we could muster enough people to scare off this terrible troll."

"I'm with you Dad," said Finn.

"I think you're both daft," said his mother. "You'll both end up as troll food."

But that night, Finn and his father packed a travelling bag, with a change of clothes and a little food, and set off. They stuck leaves to their hats so that if the troll saw them they could stand very still and sway like trees. In the dead of night they crept past the sleeping troll. They were so close, they could smell his disgusting breath as he snored. When they were safely away, they started to run.

"That was easy," they laughed.

They walked on over the mountain and when they were halfway down the other side they spied Fern's village below them, so small it looked like a neat little model. But, to their horror, they saw a monstrous hairy creature pacing up and down at the edge of the village, thumping his chest with his fists.

"Oh no!" said Finn in alarm. "Another troll."

They sat down. This was more than they had bargained for. There was a troll guarding their village and another guarding Fern's village. Now they were stuck between the two, with only enough food to last them a day.

"I bet our troll wouldn't think much of another one being so close," said Finn. "I bet they'd fight if they just happened to bump into each other."

"That's not a bad idea," said his father, jumping up. "Why don't we make sure they do bump into each other? And then we can stand back and watch them go for each other!"

Finn and his father, excited by this idea and not really thinking very sensibly, ran down the hill towards Fern's troll.

"Hey!" they shouted. "Big foot. Smelly breath. Over here!"

As they got closer, the troll stopped pacing and turned to face them with a grunt.

"This is it," cried Finn's father. "Run for your life!"

They turned and scrambled back up the mountain. The troll lumbered after them, making the ground shake with each massive footfall. Finn and his father stumbled down the other side, shouting and clapping their hands to make as much noise as possible. As they approached their own village, the other troll turned to see what all the noise was about. It let out a savage roar and galloped towards them. But then it saw the other troll crashing down the mountainside and stopped suddenly in its tracks. The two trolls looked at each other, then simultaneously let out a terrifying yell and tore towards each other.

Finn and his father slipped into a gap between two rocks and waited for the crash. It would be like two runaway wagons full of apples running into each other at full speed. They covered their heads and waited.

But the crash didn't come. Instead they heard the roaring subside into mellow grunts.

Finn peered out cautiously from his hiding place. The monsters were standing in front of each other and shuffling about nervously. One of them scratched its hairy tummy and kicked at a rock. The other snorted bashfully.

"What are they doing?" asked Finn.

"I don't know," whispered his father. "They just seem to be talking."

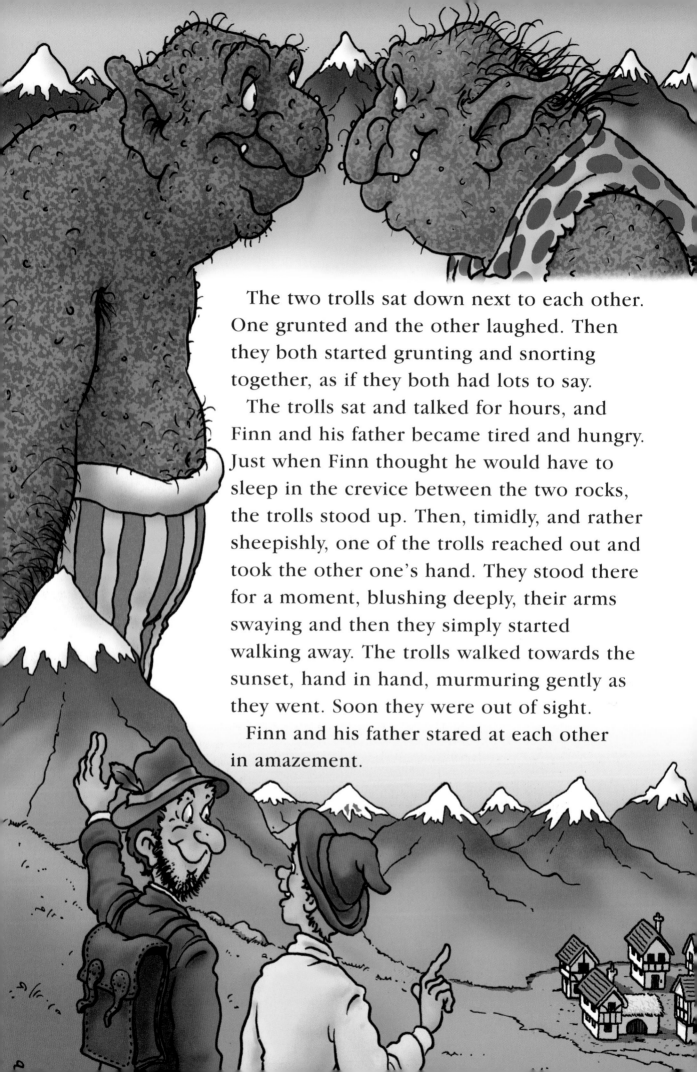

The two trolls sat down next to each other. One grunted and the other laughed. Then they both started grunting and snorting together, as if they both had lots to say.

The trolls sat and talked for hours, and Finn and his father became tired and hungry. Just when Finn thought he would have to sleep in the crevice between the two rocks, the trolls stood up. Then, timidly, and rather sheepishly, one of the trolls reached out and took the other one's hand. They stood there for a moment, blushing deeply, their arms swaying and then they simply started walking away. The trolls walked towards the sunset, hand in hand, murmuring gently as they went. Soon they were out of sight.

Finn and his father stared at each other in amazement.

"If I didn't know they were cruel, foul-smelling, people-eating nasties," said Finn's father, "I'd say those two have fallen in love."

Father and son walked down to the village, arriving just as it was getting dark. There was much laughter and cheering on the village green. The villagers had seen everything and they came out to welcome the heroes.

"I think it's wonderful," said Fern's auntie. "It just goes to show you that there's someone for everyone and that even foul-tempered trolls can find love in this world."

But Fern had an unpleasant thought...

"Does this mean that they will live happily in the mountains and then they'll have babies," she said, gulping nervously, "and then we'll hear the thump of little hairy feet?"

Now, there's a thought to leave you with!

Captain Moneybags and Lightfingers the Sea Monster

Captain Moneybags stood on board the deck of his boat, The Greedy Swindler, and looked through his telescope. Still no sight of land. They had been sailing now for five long weeks and food supplies were getting low. He looked again at his map, checked his compass and glanced at the sun. They were travelling at full sail, with the wind behind them. The skies were clear, the sea was calm – they should have reached land weeks ago. He turned to the parrot on his shoulder, and looked at her with his good eye.

"What do you think, Polly?"

"Too much dough means we go slow!" remarked Polly, wisely. Captain Moneybags knew just what she meant. Lately he had been doing rather well for himself in his chosen profession as a bold and fearless pirate, roaming the seven seas in search of buried treasure. Rather too well, in fact. Over the last few months he had loaded his ship with so many heavy wooden chests filled with gems and jewels and so many sacks stuffed with gold coins that there was barely space to move on board. Indeed, more than half the crew had been made to walk the plank recently in order to make room for it all, and yet still the greedy Captain hungered for more. But all that weight on board made the mighty ship creak and groan in the water, barely able to drag itself forward through the waves. The remaining crew had begun to mutter amongst themselves that if the Captain loaded any more booty onto the ship she was sure to keel over. Not to mention the fact they were taking bets on who would be next down the plank

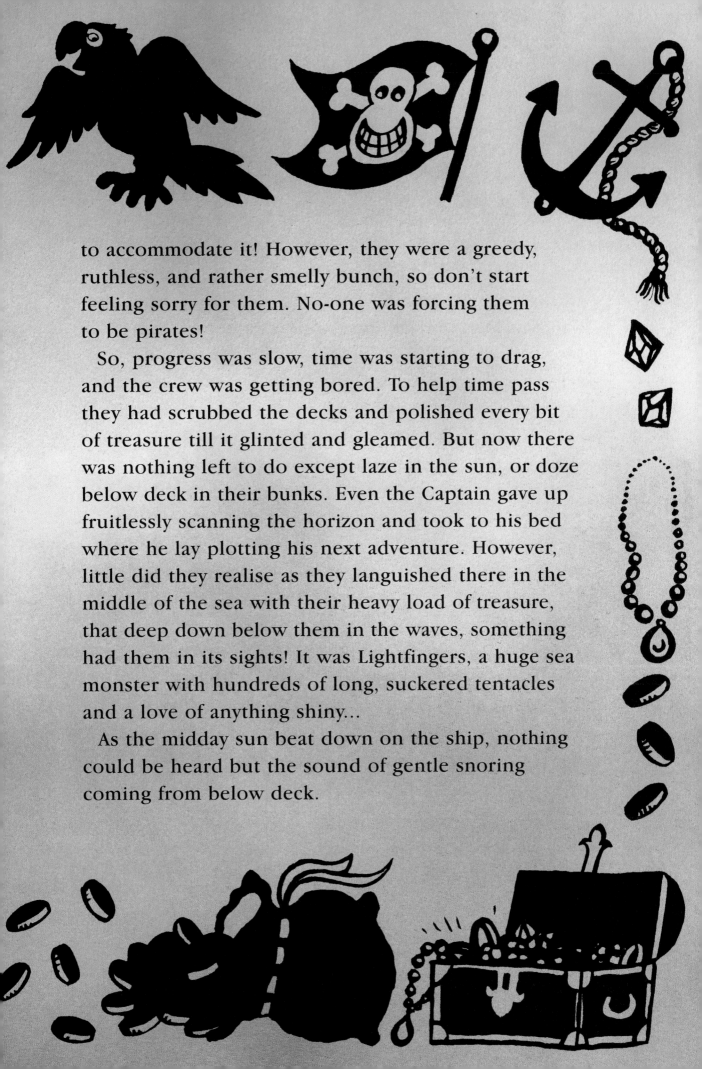

to accommodate it! However, they were a greedy, ruthless, and rather smelly bunch, so don't start feeling sorry for them. No-one was forcing them to be pirates!

So, progress was slow, time was starting to drag, and the crew was getting bored. To help time pass they had scrubbed the decks and polished every bit of treasure till it glinted and gleamed. But now there was nothing left to do except laze in the sun, or doze below deck in their bunks. Even the Captain gave up fruitlessly scanning the horizon and took to his bed where he lay plotting his next adventure. However, little did they realise as they languished there in the middle of the sea with their heavy load of treasure, that deep down below them in the waves, something had them in its sights! It was Lightfingers, a huge sea monster with hundreds of long, suckered tentacles and a love of anything shiny...

As the midday sun beat down on the ship, nothing could be heard but the sound of gentle snoring coming from below deck.

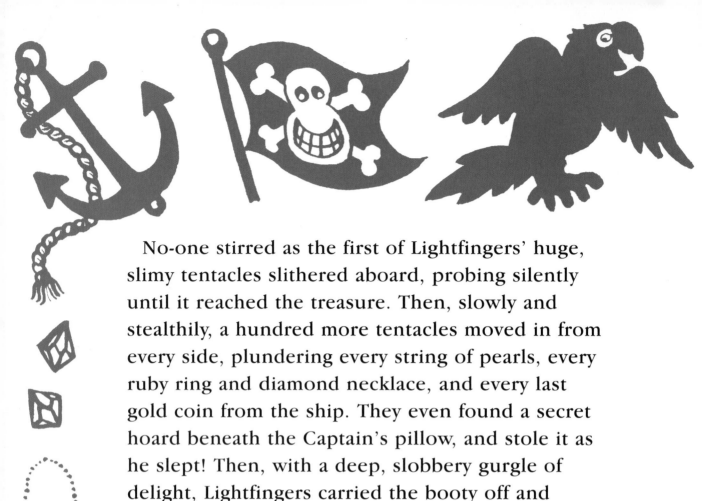

No-one stirred as the first of Lightfingers' huge, slimy tentacles slithered aboard, probing silently until it reached the treasure. Then, slowly and stealthily, a hundred more tentacles moved in from every side, plundering every string of pearls, every ruby ring and diamond necklace, and every last gold coin from the ship. They even found a secret hoard beneath the Captain's pillow, and stole it as he slept! Then, with a deep, slobbery gurgle of delight, Lightfingers carried the booty off and stashed it in his murky lair, deep in the darkest depths of the ocean.

Several hours later, the Captain awoke to the cries and moans of the crew, who had discovered the treasure mysteriously vanished into thin air and were beside themselves with grief.

"Shiver me timbers!" cried the Captain, furiously. "Treasure doesn't just vanish! Someone's hidden it! You'll walk the plank, every last one of you, unless someone tells me where it's gone!"

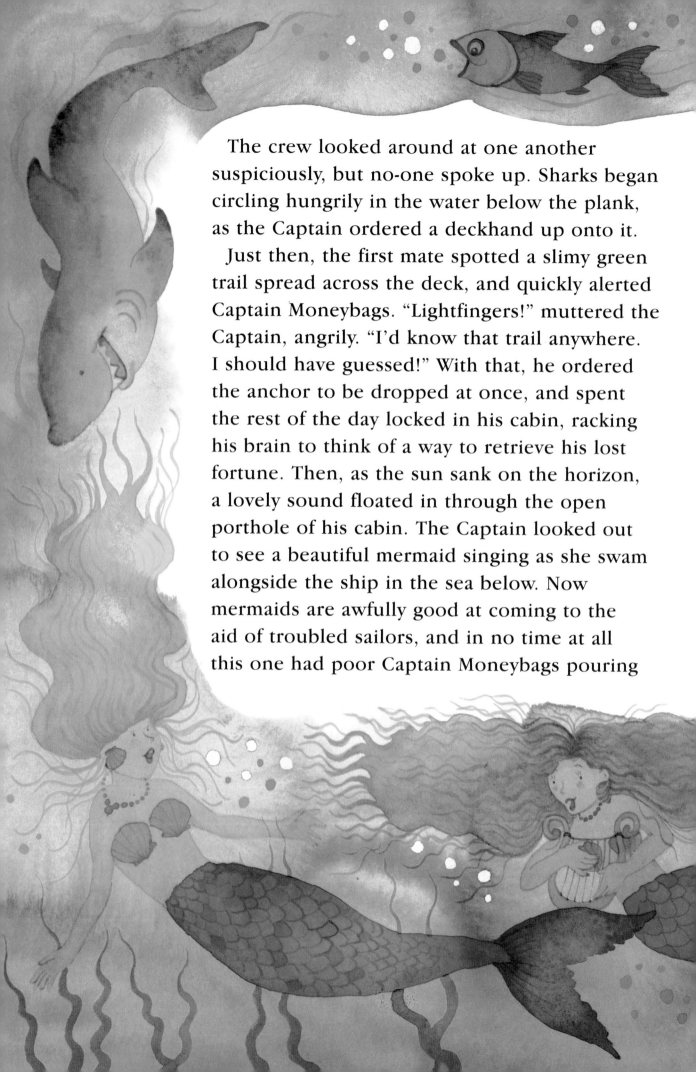

The crew looked around at one another suspiciously, but no-one spoke up. Sharks began circling hungrily in the water below the plank, as the Captain ordered a deckhand up onto it.

Just then, the first mate spotted a slimy green trail spread across the deck, and quickly alerted Captain Moneybags. "Lightfingers!" muttered the Captain, angrily. "I'd know that trail anywhere. I should have guessed!" With that, he ordered the anchor to be dropped at once, and spent the rest of the day locked in his cabin, racking his brain to think of a way to retrieve his lost fortune. Then, as the sun sank on the horizon, a lovely sound floated in through the open porthole of his cabin. The Captain looked out to see a beautiful mermaid singing as she swam alongside the ship in the sea below. Now mermaids are awfully good at coming to the aid of troubled sailors, and in no time at all this one had poor Captain Moneybags pouring

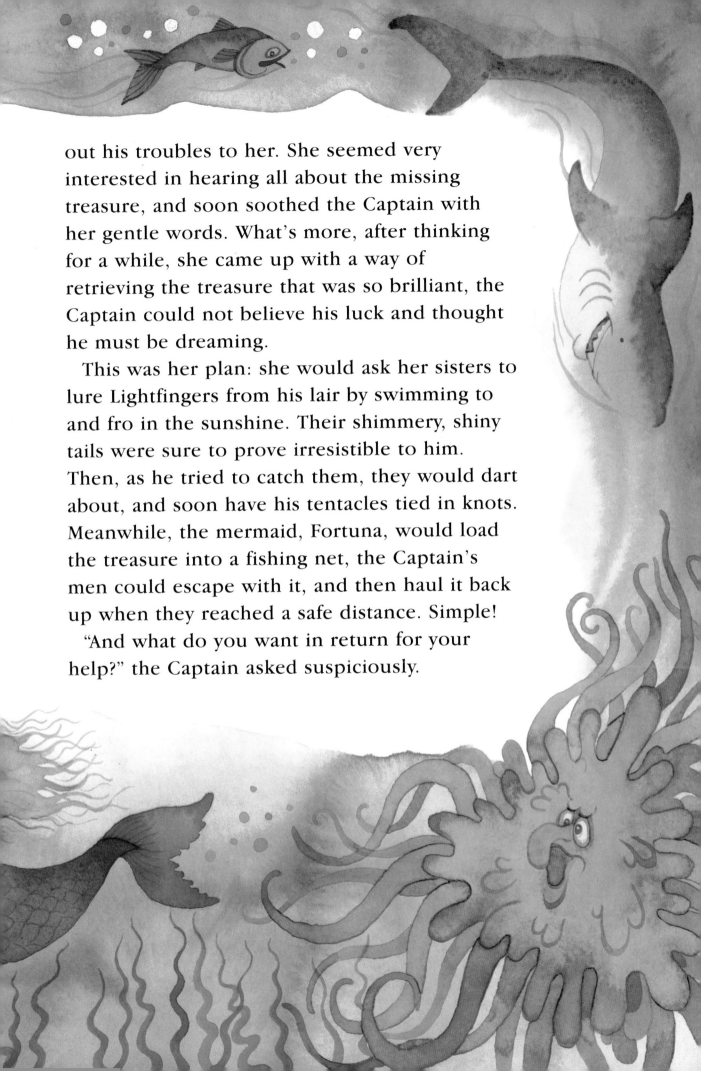

out his troubles to her. She seemed very interested in hearing all about the missing treasure, and soon soothed the Captain with her gentle words. What's more, after thinking for a while, she came up with a way of retrieving the treasure that was so brilliant, the Captain could not believe his luck and thought he must be dreaming.

This was her plan: she would ask her sisters to lure Lightfingers from his lair by swimming to and fro in the sunshine. Their shimmery, shiny tails were sure to prove irresistible to him. Then, as he tried to catch them, they would dart about, and soon have his tentacles tied in knots. Meanwhile, the mermaid, Fortuna, would load the treasure into a fishing net, the Captain's men could escape with it, and then haul it back up when they reached a safe distance. Simple!

"And what do you want in return for your help?" the Captain asked suspiciously.

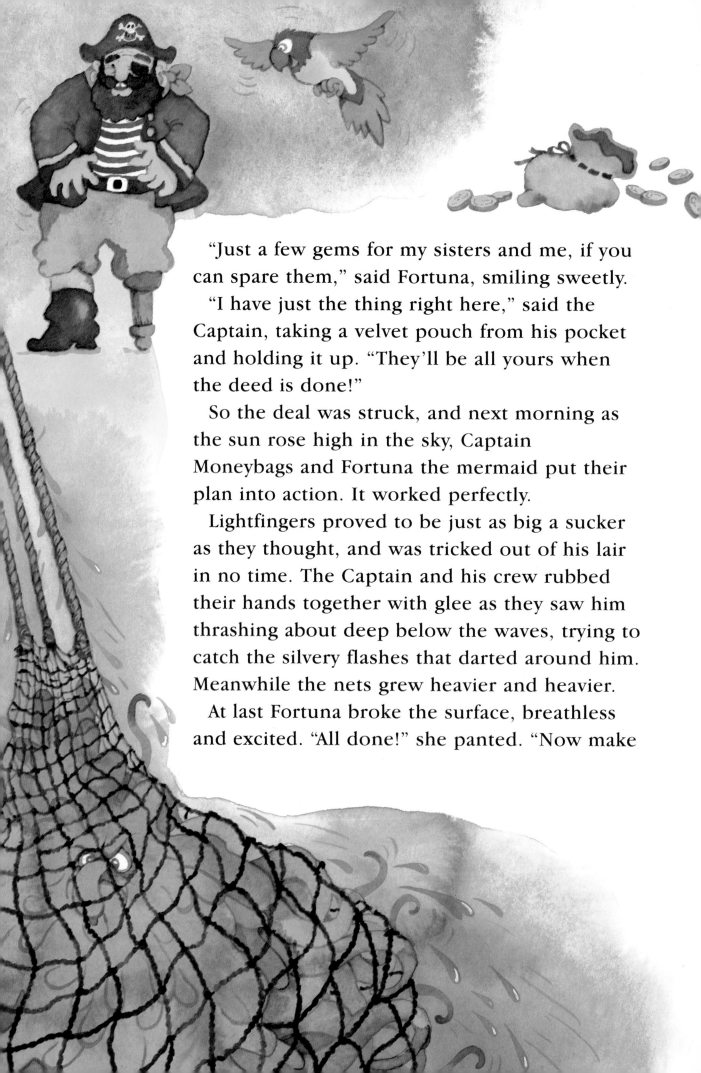

"Just a few gems for my sisters and me, if you can spare them," said Fortuna, smiling sweetly.

"I have just the thing right here," said the Captain, taking a velvet pouch from his pocket and holding it up. "They'll be all yours when the deed is done!"

So the deal was struck, and next morning as the sun rose high in the sky, Captain Moneybags and Fortuna the mermaid put their plan into action. It worked perfectly.

Lightfingers proved to be just as big a sucker as they thought, and was tricked out of his lair in no time. The Captain and his crew rubbed their hands together with glee as they saw him thrashing about deep below the waves, trying to catch the silvery flashes that darted around him. Meanwhile the nets grew heavier and heavier.

At last Fortuna broke the surface, breathless and excited. "All done!" she panted. "Now make

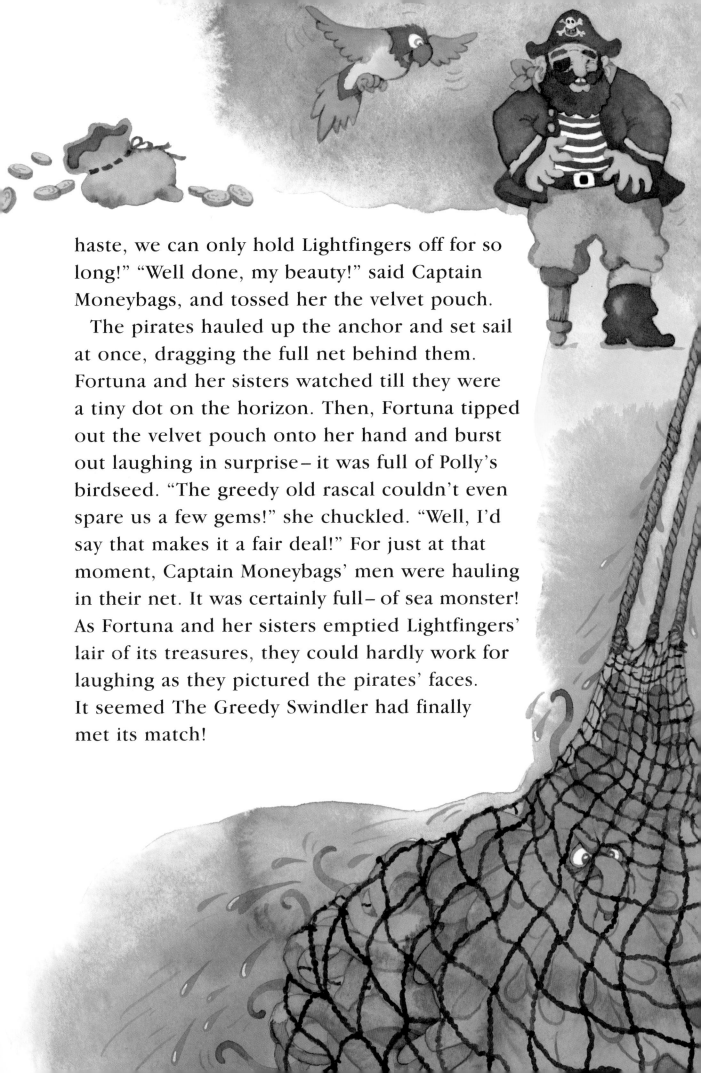

haste, we can only hold Lightfingers off for so long!" "Well done, my beauty!" said Captain Moneybags, and tossed her the velvet pouch.

The pirates hauled up the anchor and set sail at once, dragging the full net behind them. Fortuna and her sisters watched till they were a tiny dot on the horizon. Then, Fortuna tipped out the velvet pouch onto her hand and burst out laughing in surprise – it was full of Polly's birdseed. "The greedy old rascal couldn't even spare us a few gems!" she chuckled. "Well, I'd say that makes it a fair deal!" For just at that moment, Captain Moneybags' men were hauling in their net. It was certainly full – of sea monster! As Fortuna and her sisters emptied Lightfingers' lair of its treasures, they could hardly work for laughing as they pictured the pirates' faces. It seemed The Greedy Swindler had finally met its match!

DINOS

MENU

Dino's Chips
Diplodocus Dips
Caveman's Lunch
Stegosaurus Steak
Brontosaurus Brunch
Deep Fried Lizard
Mammoth Milkshake
Surprise Dish of the Day...

Dino's

There's a prehistoric venue
That's open day and night.
With a megasaurus menu
For the larger appetite.

Try their Stegosaurus Steak
Or Brontosaurus Brunch,
A massive Mammoth Milkshake
Or the three course Caveman's Lunch.

Triceratops call in to try
The Diplodocus dips.
Pterodactyls leave the sky
For Dino's famous chips.

Raptors are enraptured
By the tasty Deep-fried Lizard –
Each one freshly captured
By the culinary wizard.

For the best in haute cuisine
Nowhere could be finer.
It's the place you should be seen,
It's Dino's Downtown Diner.

So grant the dinosaur his wish
And come and join the queue.
You're sure to like his 'special' dish,
Why? Because it's YOU!

The Lost Valley

Deep in the hot and steamy, green jungle far away from busy cities, or even quiet little villages, there was a secret valley. Tucked away in a great gorge and watered by a mighty river that flowed over the jagged cliffs surrounding it, the valley had lain undisturbed since life on earth began.

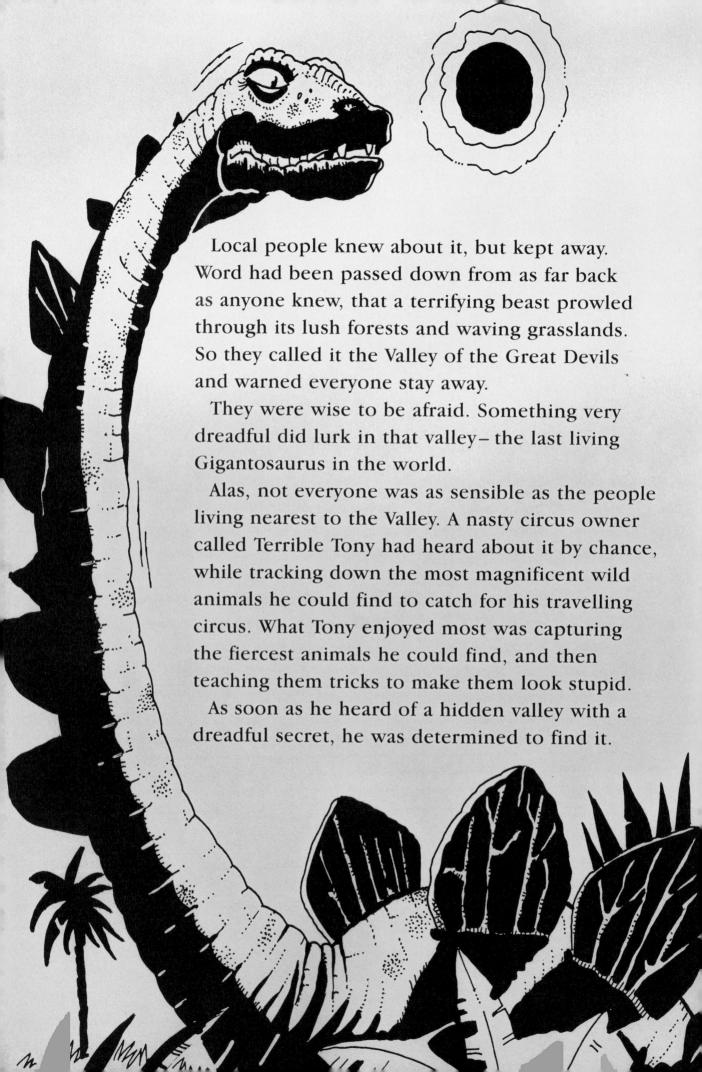

Local people knew about it, but kept away.
Word had been passed down from as far back
as anyone knew, that a terrifying beast prowled
through its lush forests and waving grasslands.
So they called it the Valley of the Great Devils
and warned everyone stay away.

They were wise to be afraid. Something very
dreadful did lurk in that valley – the last living
Gigantosaurus in the world.

Alas, not everyone was as sensible as the people
living nearest to the Valley. A nasty circus owner
called Terrible Tony had heard about it by chance,
while tracking down the most magnificent wild
animals he could find to catch for his travelling
circus. What Tony enjoyed most was capturing
the fiercest animals he could find, and then
teaching them tricks to make them look stupid.

As soon as he heard of a hidden valley with a
dreadful secret, he was determined to find it.

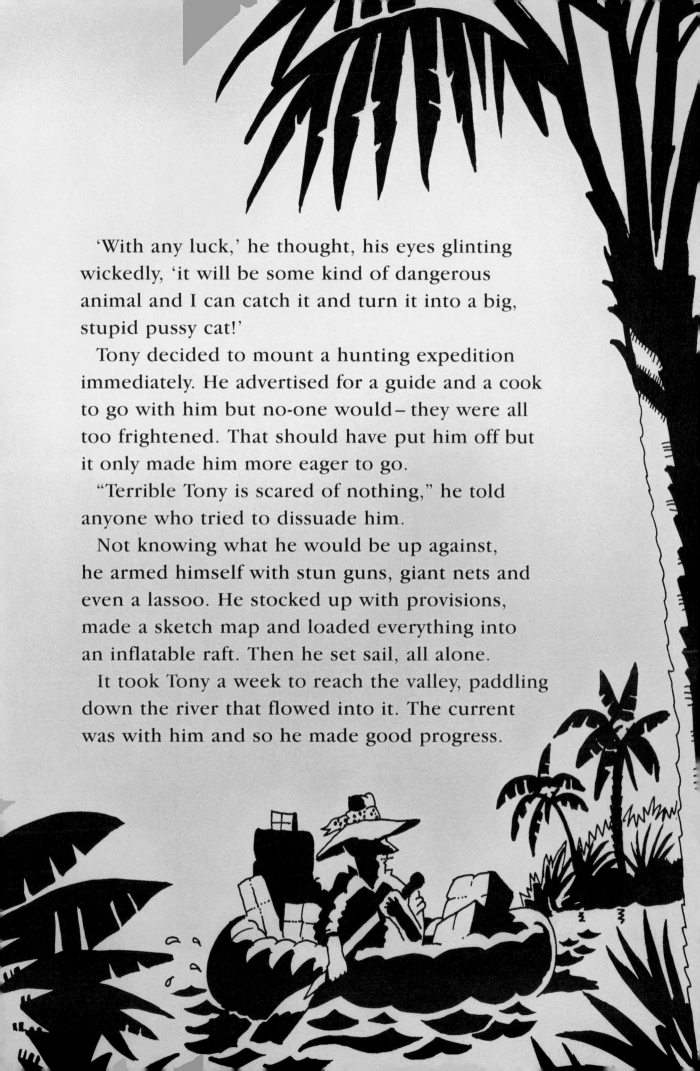

'With any luck,' he thought, his eyes glinting wickedly, 'it will be some kind of dangerous animal and I can catch it and turn it into a big, stupid pussy cat!'

Tony decided to mount a hunting expedition immediately. He advertised for a guide and a cook to go with him but no-one would – they were all too frightened. That should have put him off but it only made him more eager to go.

"Terrible Tony is scared of nothing," he told anyone who tried to dissuade him.

Not knowing what he would be up against, he armed himself with stun guns, giant nets and even a lassoo. He stocked up with provisions, made a sketch map and loaded everything into an inflatable raft. Then he set sail, all alone.

It took Tony a week to reach the valley, paddling down the river that flowed into it. The current was with him and so he made good progress.

The further he travelled into the jungle, the
wilder it became. Often, he couldn't see the sky
at all through the thick canopy of leaves overhead.
The air was full of noises. Parrots squawked and
monkeys chattered in the trees around him.
Elephants trumpeted from the banks and
crocodiles snapped at him.

Then, one morning, Tony heard a very different
sound – a bloodcurdling roar. All the animal
noises stopped and there was an eerie silence.

"Pipe down, pussycat," Tony shouted, paddling
even faster.

No-one else had ventured into the valley, they
had just looked down from the top of the
mountainous gorge on either side. Tony had been
told that the river flowed through it but he had
no idea that it crashed down over huge boulders.

Descending into the valley was like doing the
scariest water ride imaginable again and again.

One moment he was paddling along, and the next he was nose-diving over the edge of sheer rock. The last waterfall was the worst of all. It was so steep that the raft took off. As Tony clung on desperately, he sailed over the tree tops before coming to land in one of the shallow pits that criss-crossed a lush plain. There was something odd about the shape and pattern of those pits, then Tony realised what they were – giant footprints!

Even though each print was wide and deep enough to hold his entire raft, he was still sure that whatever the creature was, it would be no match for him. Foolish Tony *still* wasn't worried!

The earth began to shudder – something was coming that was so enormous, it was making the ground shake.

The trees parted and a giant lizard burst out of the jungle. It was as long as a town square and as tall as a skyscraper. It was the rarest creature in the world, the last of a long line of Gigantosauri that had lived in the valley since every other dinosaur had become extinct.

If Tony had had any sense, he would have run for his life.

Instead he yelled. "Over here stupid!"

The Gigantosaurus couldn't hear him. Tony's shouts sounded like tiny, far away squeaks. However, it had spotted the bright orange raft and made straight for it.

The enormous creature stopped just before it reached the raft and sniffed the air. Then it opened its huge jaws and gave a terrific, earsplitting roar.

"You don't scare me, you big, overgrown alligator!" shouted Tony, guessing the monster had scented him. The Gigantosaurus threw back its head and bellowed so loudly that the sound echoed through the jungle like thunder and the villagers shook in their shoes. Tony fired a round of darts from his stun gun at the huge reptile and waited for it to keel over unconscious, so that he could tie it up.

But instead the Gigantosaurus just shook itself lazily as all the tranquillised darts fell harmlessly to the ground. It studied the tiny red-faced creature which was making such a horrible noise, when it should have fallen silent in the presence of the King of the Valley. Then it took action to remove it.

Swiftly, it bent down and seized Tony in its mighty jaws. But the Gigantosaurus didn't

swallow him in a single gulp. It reared up
on its hind legs until it was as tall as two
skyscrapers, and tossed him away. Then it
picked up the raft and hurled it after him.

Tony flew out of the valley and over the
hills beyond. Luckily for him, he landed,
unharmed, with an almighty splash in a
distant lagoon and a few moments later, his
raft hit the water right beside him.

Tony paddled across that lagoon to the
town on its banks as fast as he could go.
Then he hailed a taxi to the airport, boarded
a plane and never, ever came back.

Meeting that monster changed Tony forever.
He shut down his circus and released all the
animals safely back into the wild. He made a
lot of friends for the first time in his life.

And the Gigantosaurus lived happily ever
afterwards in his Valley.

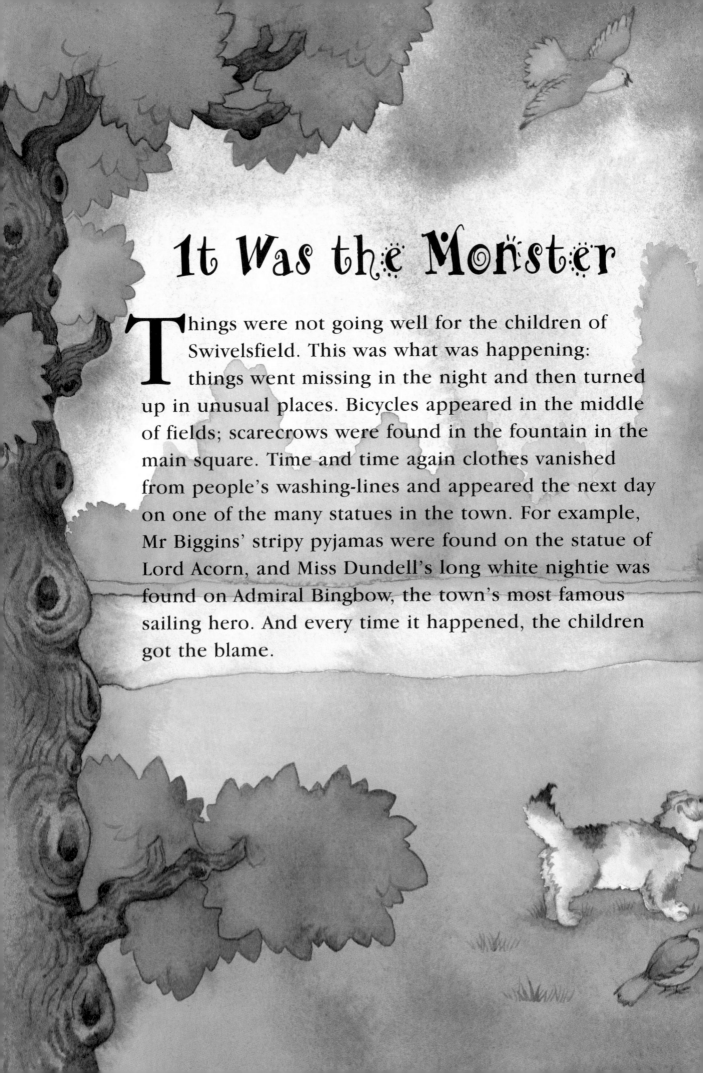

It Was the Monster

Things were not going well for the children of Swivelsfield. This was what was happening: things went missing in the night and then turned up in unusual places. Bicycles appeared in the middle of fields; scarecrows were found in the fountain in the main square. Time and time again clothes vanished from people's washing-lines and appeared the next day on one of the many statues in the town. For example, Mr Biggins' stripy pyjamas were found on the statue of Lord Acorn, and Miss Dundell's long white nightie was found on Admiral Bingbow, the town's most famous sailing hero. And every time it happened, the children got the blame.

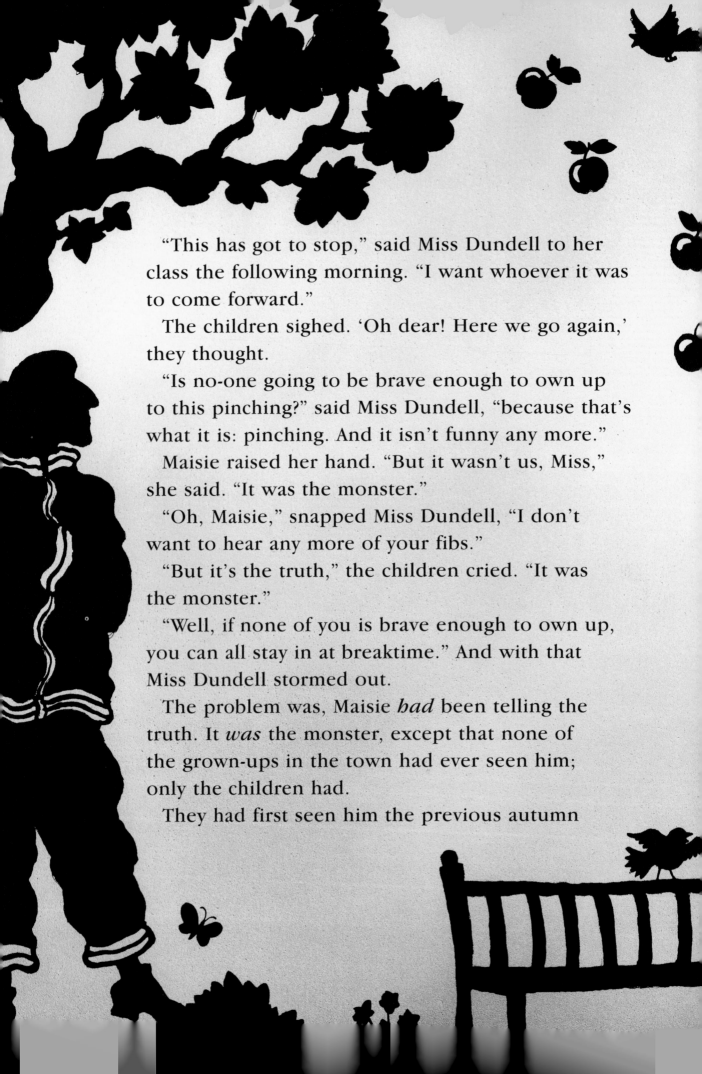

"This has got to stop," said Miss Dundell to her class the following morning. "I want whoever it was to come forward."

The children sighed. 'Oh dear! Here we go again,' they thought.

"Is no-one going to be brave enough to own up to this pinching?" said Miss Dundell, "because that's what it is: pinching. And it isn't funny any more."

Maisie raised her hand. "But it wasn't us, Miss," she said. "It was the monster."

"Oh, Maisie," snapped Miss Dundell, "I don't want to hear any more of your fibs."

"But it's the truth," the children cried. "It was the monster."

"Well, if none of you is brave enough to own up, you can all stay in at breaktime." And with that Miss Dundell stormed out.

The problem was, Maisie *had* been telling the truth. It *was* the monster, except that none of the grown-ups in the town had ever seen him; only the children had.

They had first seen him the previous autumn

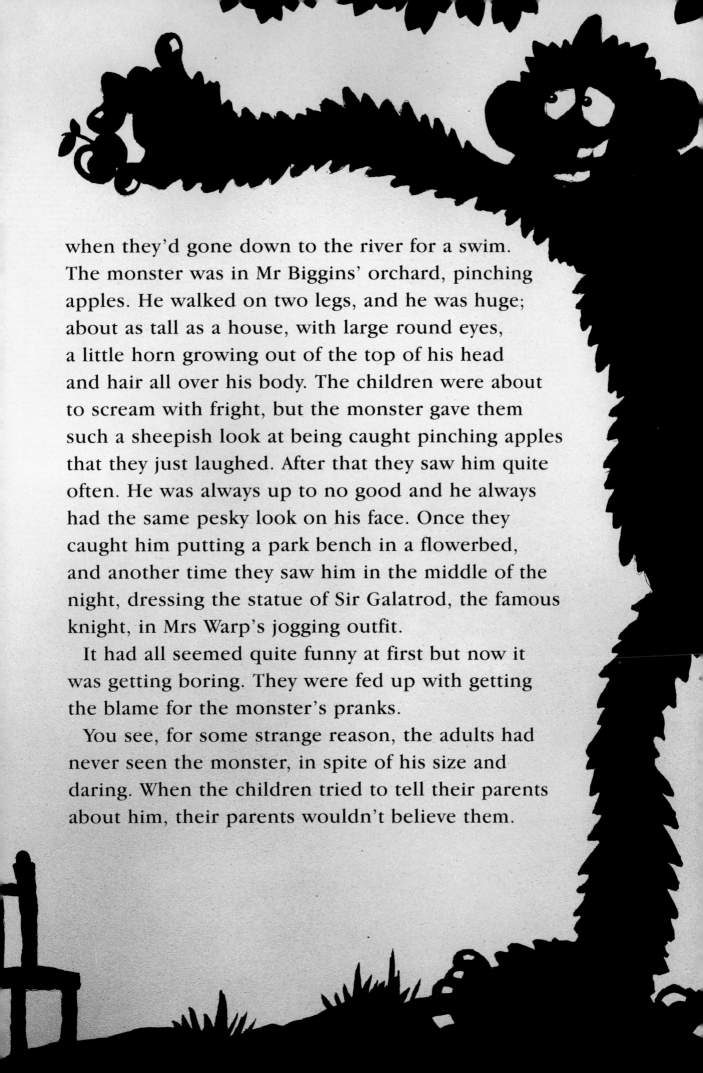

when they'd gone down to the river for a swim.
The monster was in Mr Biggins' orchard, pinching
apples. He walked on two legs, and he was huge;
about as tall as a house, with large round eyes,
a little horn growing out of the top of his head
and hair all over his body. The children were about
to scream with fright, but the monster gave them
such a sheepish look at being caught pinching apples
that they just laughed. After that they saw him quite
often. He was always up to no good and he always
had the same pesky look on his face. Once they
caught him putting a park bench in a flowerbed,
and another time they saw him in the middle of the
night, dressing the statue of Sir Galatrod, the famous
knight, in Mrs Warp's jogging outfit.

It had all seemed quite funny at first but now it
was getting boring. They were fed up with getting
the blame for the monster's pranks.

You see, for some strange reason, the adults had
never seen the monster, in spite of his size and
daring. When the children tried to tell their parents
about him, their parents wouldn't believe them.

Maisie came up with a plan.

"What we've got to do," she said to the class, "is trick the monster into doing something we couldn't possibly do ourselves. That way our parents will believe us."

"But what?" asked Mac.

"Well," continued Maisie, "the monster's favourite prank is dressing up statues, which we could easily do. But there's one statue that's too big for us to reach, even with ladders– the statue of the Queen in the main square. If we could trick the monster into dressing up that statue, he'll give himself away."

"But the Queen's statue is huge," said Jules. "Where will we find clothes that are big enough?"

"We'll make some," said Maisie.

And that's what they did. Maisie's mum owned a fabric shop so they had lots of pieces of fabric to use.

"Let's make a clown's outfit," suggested Mac.

The children got together in teams to make the clothes they needed: one for the giant hat, another for the oversized trousers and so on. They worked hard over the next few days and on the eve of the Queen's birthday celebrations, the clown's costume was ready.

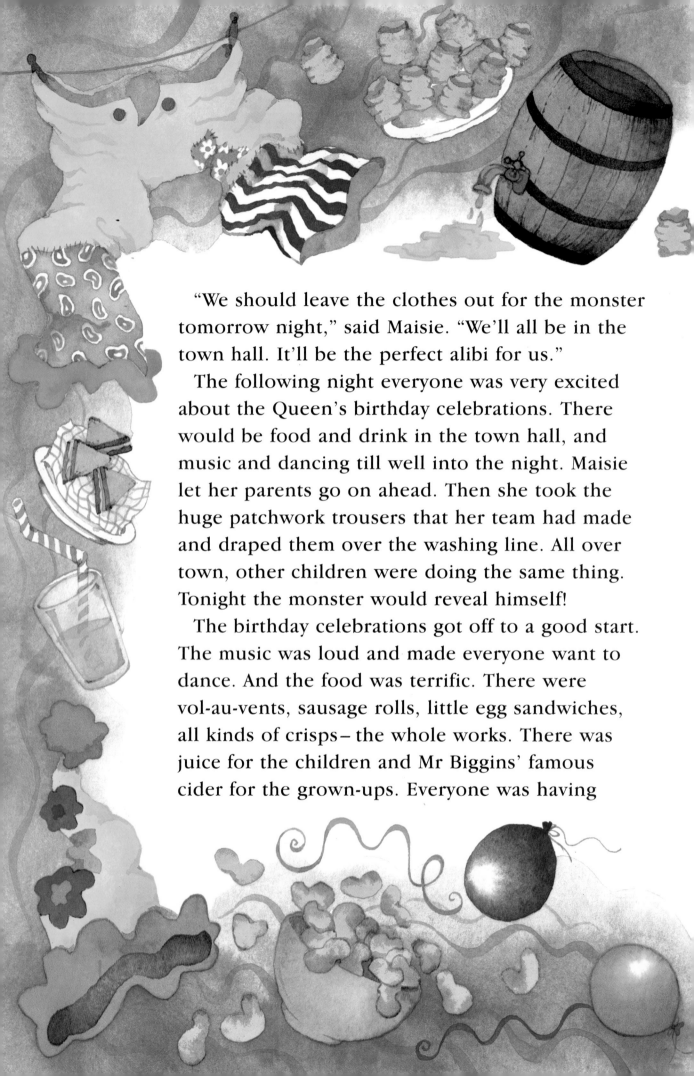

"We should leave the clothes out for the monster tomorrow night," said Maisie. "We'll all be in the town hall. It'll be the perfect alibi for us."

The following night everyone was very excited about the Queen's birthday celebrations. There would be food and drink in the town hall, and music and dancing till well into the night. Maisie let her parents go on ahead. Then she took the huge patchwork trousers that her team had made and draped them over the washing line. All over town, other children were doing the same thing. Tonight the monster would reveal himself!

The birthday celebrations got off to a good start. The music was loud and made everyone want to dance. And the food was terrific. There were vol-au-vents, sausage rolls, little egg sandwiches, all kinds of crisps – the whole works. There was juice for the children and Mr Biggins' famous cider for the grown-ups. Everyone was having

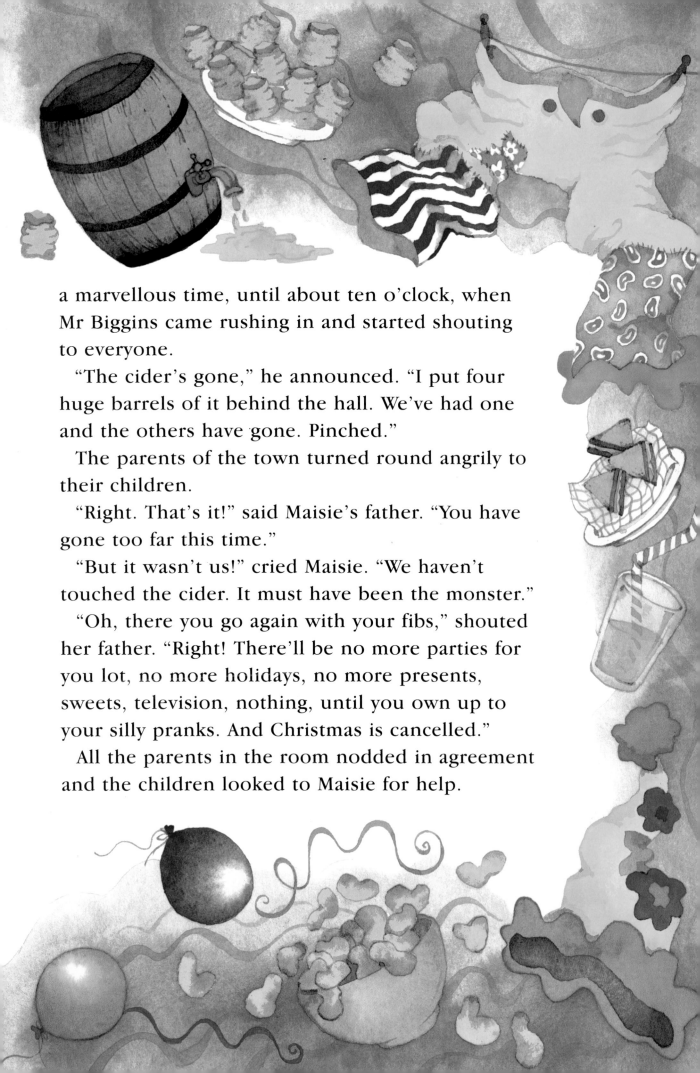

a marvellous time, until about ten o'clock, when
Mr Biggins came rushing in and started shouting
to everyone.

"The cider's gone," he announced. "I put four
huge barrels of it behind the hall. We've had one
and the others have gone. Pinched."

The parents of the town turned round angrily to
their children.

"Right. That's it!" said Maisie's father. "You have
gone too far this time."

"But it wasn't us!" cried Maisie. "We haven't
touched the cider. It must have been the monster."

"Oh, there you go again with your fibs," shouted
her father. "Right! There'll be no more parties for
you lot, no more holidays, no more presents,
sweets, television, nothing, until you own up to
your silly pranks. And Christmas is cancelled."

All the parents in the room nodded in agreement
and the children looked to Maisie for help.

"Well, if you don't believe us," said Maisie, with tears in her eyes. "just go outside and look at the statue of the Queen. The monster has dressed it up this evening while we've all been in here, and we couldn't *possibly* have done it, because, well… we're in here and we couldn't reach anyway."

Everyone trooped outside. The street lamps lit up all the streets, the main square and the giant statue of the Queen. They all looked up at the statue, and there she was, Her Majesty, tall, regal… and untouched. There was no sign of the clown costume. In the silence you could hear sobs coming from the children. No-one would ever believe them now.

But not far away, and coming closer, the townspeople could hear singing; a loud, roaring, drunken kind of singing and the sound of giant footsteps. The monster lurched round a corner and into view. Everyone gasped.

The monster staggered into the main square, singing at the top of his voice. He was swigging from a barrel of cider which he held in one great hairy paw.

The adults looked up in amazement and the children cheered, for not only had the monster drunk himself silly and finally staggered into full view of their parents – he was dressed from head to hairy foot in the giant clown's costume.

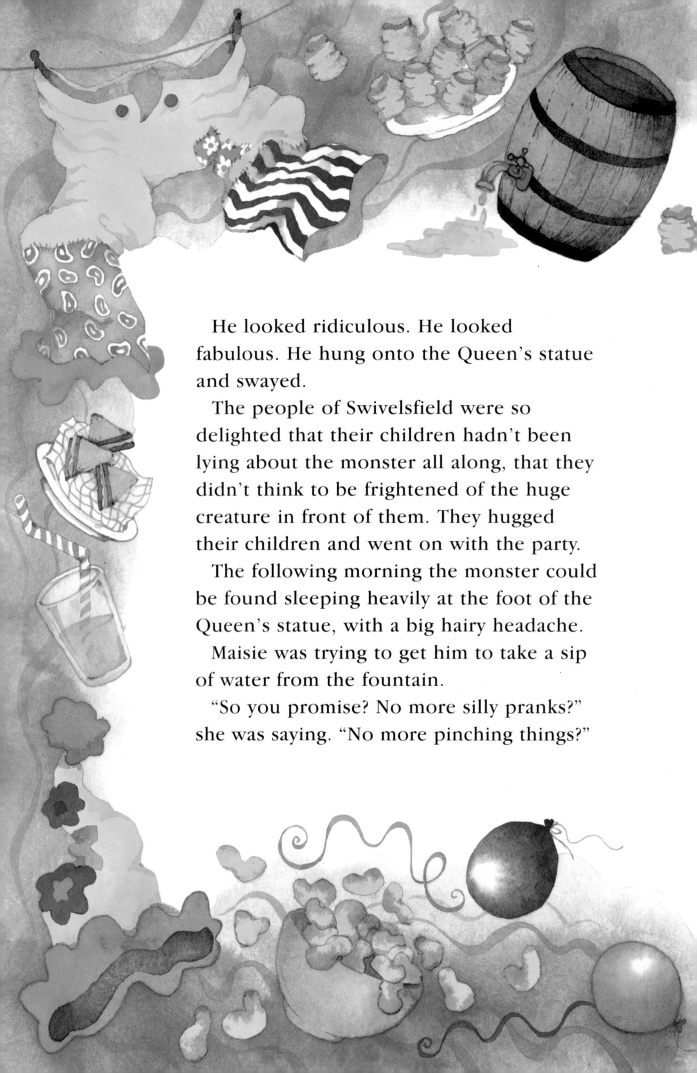

He looked ridiculous. He looked fabulous. He hung onto the Queen's statue and swayed.

The people of Swivelsfield were so delighted that their children hadn't been lying about the monster all along, that they didn't think to be frightened of the huge creature in front of them. They hugged their children and went on with the party.

The following morning the monster could be found sleeping heavily at the foot of the Queen's statue, with a big hairy headache.

Maisie was trying to get him to take a sip of water from the fountain.

"So you promise? No more silly pranks?" she was saying. "No more pinching things?"

The monster nodded and groaned. "Instead you could do useful things," she continued. "Help us to pick the apples, put up the Christmas decorations, all sorts of things." The monster groaned and smiled sheepishly.

Maisie ran back home. There were so many things to look forward to: holidays, presents, sweets, Christmas... and a huge, hairy, friendly monster to play with. The future suddenly looked great!

Mystery Monster

Y ou wake with a start,
In the still of the night,
With your toes all exposed,
And your quilt pulled up tight.

With a terrible feeling
Of doom and unease,
That thumps in your heart,
And knocks at your knees.

You open your eyes,
You stare through the gloom,
Strange shadows loom large,
On the walls of your room.

You hear a loud creak,
As the monster draws near,
And the more that you listen,
The more that you hear.

Then you see its weird shape,
At the end of your bed,
With long skinny legs,
And a great lumpy head.

So you switch on the light,
And you whisper, "Who's there?"
But it's only your clothes,
Hanging over the chair.

Princess Prissy and the Stinky Bog Monster

King Fusspot liked everything to be just so. Every corner of his palace was kept neat and shiny as a new pin. Each morning before breakfast he would stand at the top of the sweeping staircase that led down into the great hall, and take a royal roll call of his entire household. If anyone was so much as one second late, they would spend the rest of the day polishing the silver.

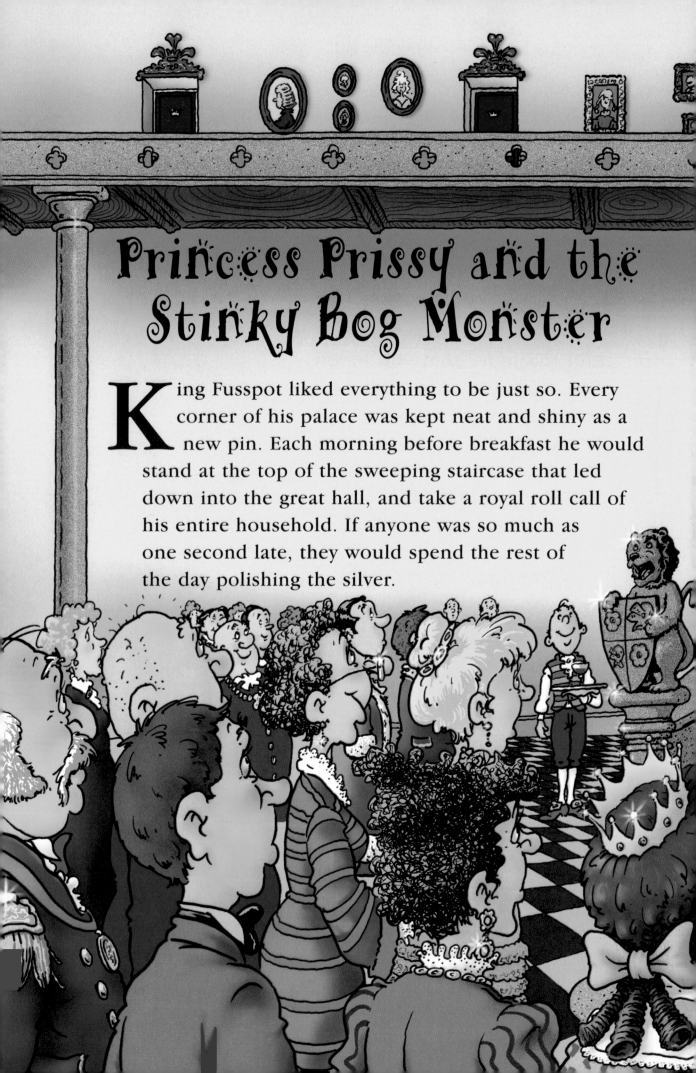

And that was not all. The King had rules that were written in his Rule Book, a volume so heavy that three footmen were needed to lift it. Woe betide anyone who broke his rules.

So, there was a place for everything, and everything (and everyone) was in its place. And as long as no-one stepped out of line, they all lived happily and peacefully together.

Then one morning, as King Fusspot stood at the top of the staircase as usual, taking his roll call, something most irregular happened. He had ticked the Queen and his three eldest daughters off in his register, but when he came to his youngest daughter, Princess Prissy, there was no reply!

"Princess Prissy," he called again. No answer. "Confound it all! Where is she?" demanded the King. "This is most unlike her."

And indeed it was, for Princess Prissy was a proper little chip off the old block. She went so far as to have her own Rule Book, covering such pressing matters as the number of brushstrokes that royal hair should receive before bed,

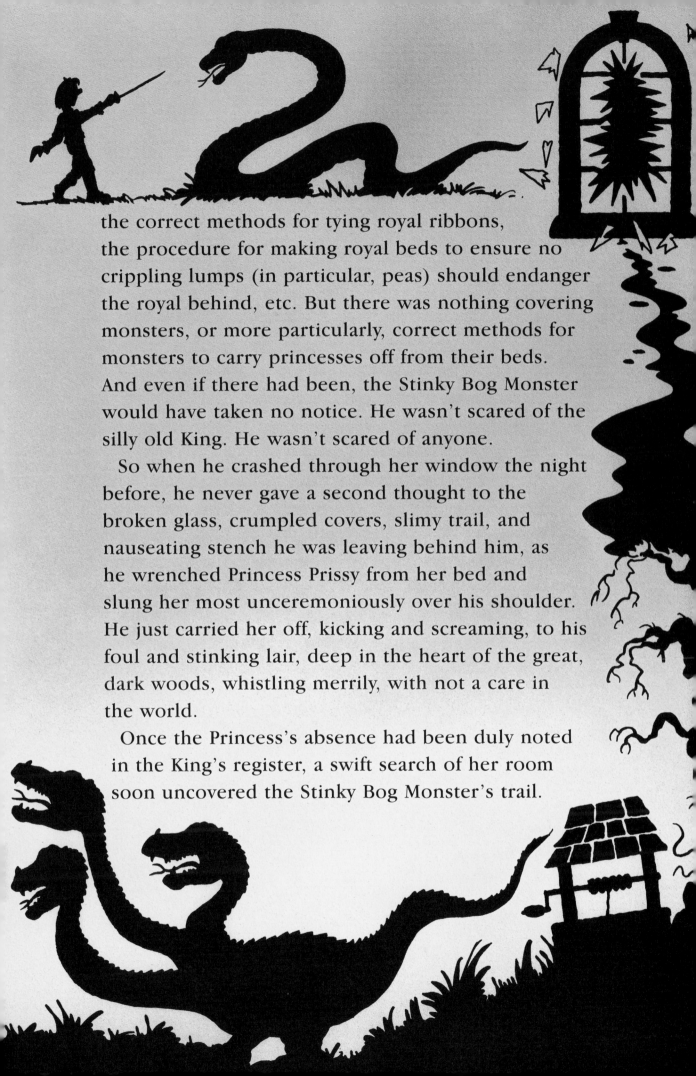

the correct methods for tying royal ribbons,
the procedure for making royal beds to ensure no
crippling lumps (in particular, peas) should endanger
the royal behind, etc. But there was nothing covering
monsters, or more particularly, correct methods for
monsters to carry princesses off from their beds.
And even if there had been, the Stinky Bog Monster
would have taken no notice. He wasn't scared of the
silly old King. He wasn't scared of anyone.

So when he crashed through her window the night
before, he never gave a second thought to the
broken glass, crumpled covers, slimy trail, and
nauseating stench he was leaving behind him, as
he wrenched Princess Prissy from her bed and
slung her most unceremoniously over his shoulder.
He just carried her off, kicking and screaming, to his
foul and stinking lair, deep in the heart of the great,
dark woods, whistling merrily, with not a care in
the world.

Once the Princess's absence had been duly noted
in the King's register, a swift search of her room
soon uncovered the Stinky Bog Monster's trail.

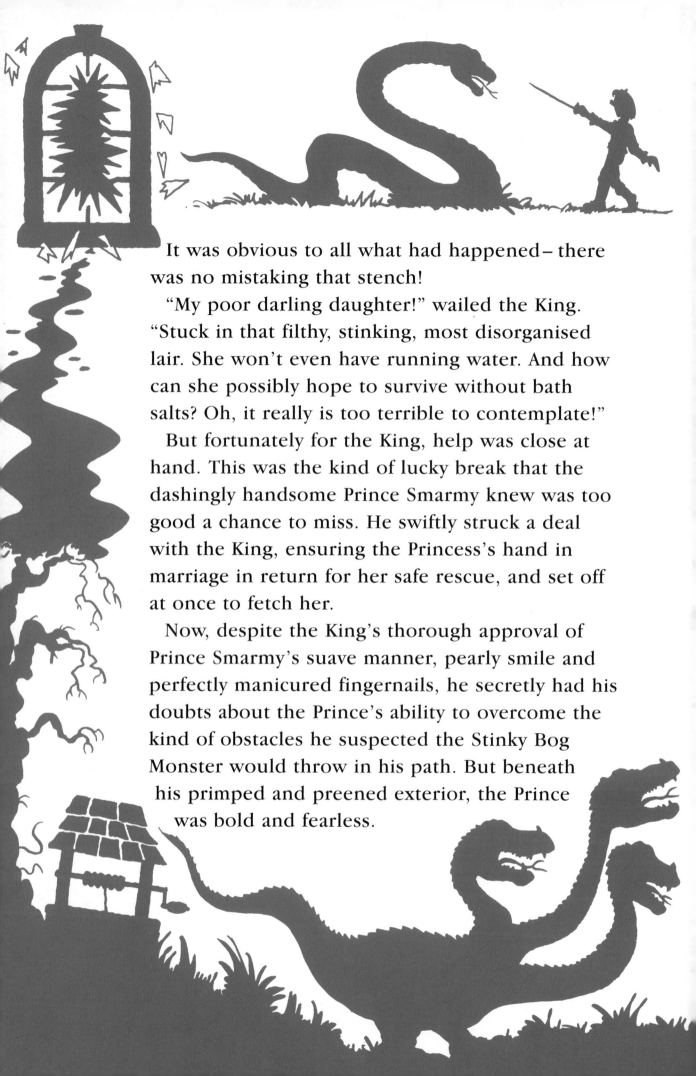

It was obvious to all what had happened – there was no mistaking that stench!

"My poor darling daughter!" wailed the King. "Stuck in that filthy, stinking, most disorganised lair. She won't even have running water. And how can she possibly hope to survive without bath salts? Oh, it really is too terrible to contemplate!"

But fortunately for the King, help was close at hand. This was the kind of lucky break that the dashingly handsome Prince Smarmy knew was too good a chance to miss. He swiftly struck a deal with the King, ensuring the Princess's hand in marriage in return for her safe rescue, and set off at once to fetch her.

Now, despite the King's thorough approval of Prince Smarmy's suave manner, pearly smile and perfectly manicured fingernails, he secretly had his doubts about the Prince's ability to overcome the kind of obstacles he suspected the Stinky Bog Monster would throw in his path. But beneath his primped and preened exterior, the Prince was bold and fearless.

What is more, he was absolutely crackers about Princess Prissy, so he was not about to let anything stand in his way.

Deep in the heart of the great, dark woods, Prince Smarmy had to battle his way past demons and dragons, vampires and vipers, ogres and trolls to reach the Stinky Bog Monster's lair.

"No problem," smirked the Prince smugly, brushing himself down after a rather unpleasant encounter with a three-headed beast. And before long, he arrived at the entrance to the Stinky Bog Monster's loathsome lair itself! Now all he had to do was retrieve the Princess, whisk her back to the palace, and he'd be home, safe and up the aisle in no time.

However, Prince Smarmy, unlike the Stinky Bog Monster, was quite familiar with the Princess's Rule Book (not to mention the King's) and knew all the proper procedures to follow

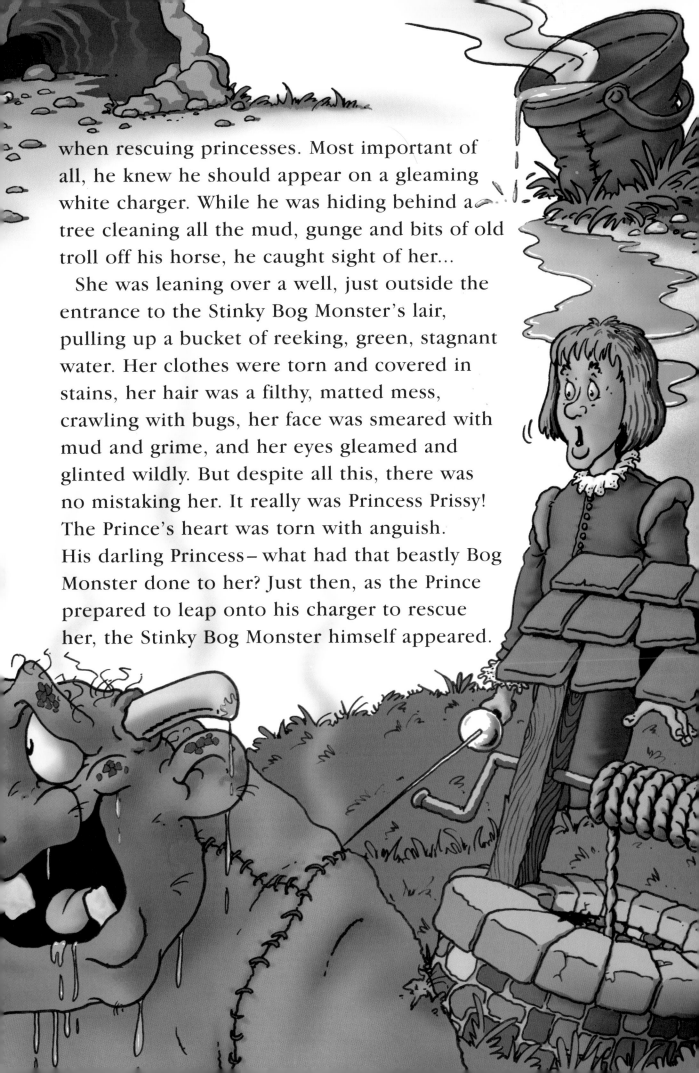

when rescuing princesses. Most important of all, he knew he should appear on a gleaming white charger. While he was hiding behind a tree cleaning all the mud, gunge and bits of old troll off his horse, he caught sight of her...

She was leaning over a well, just outside the entrance to the Stinky Bog Monster's lair, pulling up a bucket of reeking, green, stagnant water. Her clothes were torn and covered in stains, her hair was a filthy, matted mess, crawling with bugs, her face was smeared with mud and grime, and her eyes gleamed and glinted wildly. But despite all this, there was no mistaking her. It really was Princess Prissy! The Prince's heart was torn with anguish. His darling Princess— what had that beastly Bog Monster done to her? Just then, as the Prince prepared to leap onto his charger to rescue her, the Stinky Bog Monster himself appeared.

Princess Prissy turned and greeted him with a blackened, gappy smile.

"Hello there, Boggy darling! Come and smell how nice and stagnant the water is today! Our tea should taste really disgusting with this!" And with that, she reached out, took his hand and planted a slobbery kiss on his cheek! As the Prince cried out in horror, the Princess and her Bog Monster turned and caught sight of him.

"Oh, yuk, not you!" spat the Princess. "If you've come to rescue me, you can get lost, I'm not coming home – ever!"

"Don't be ridiculous Prissy," cried the horrified Prince. "You can't stay here. Look at yourself – you're hideous! He's got you hypnotised. But don't worry, you'll soon come to your senses…"

"Oh, but I have come to my senses," hissed Princess Prissy. "At last I've escaped all those silly rules. All that niceness, and prettiness, and good manners. I'm free! I like being rude and horrible

and hideous, it's really rather fun. I've got my
darling Stinky Bog Monster to thank for it, and
you're too late – we got married last night!" Then
Princess Prissy and the Bog Monster let out cackling
laughs and staggered back inside.

There was nothing else for it. Prince Smarmy
had to admit defeat, turn on his heels, and head
home. He wondered what the King would say.
It would certainly mess up his neat register. Then
he noticed a deep, muddy puddle in front of him.

'Why not?' he thought, and rode his clean,
white horse straight through it, splattering both
of them with black, sticky mud. Then he saw
another one. This time he made his horse jump
into it. He laughed out loud.

'You never know,' he thought. 'Perhaps the
Princess was right, after all. Perhaps some rules
are just too silly.'

And he rode through every single puddle until
he got back to the castle.

The Fantastic Firework

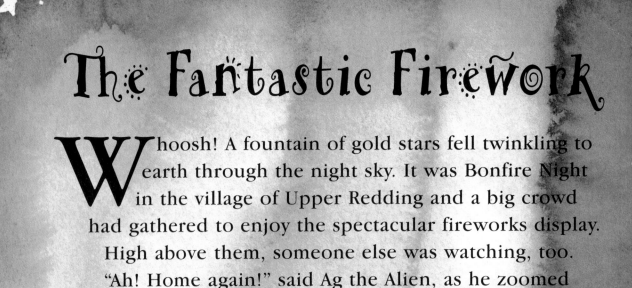

Whoosh! A fountain of gold stars fell twinkling to earth through the night sky. It was Bonfire Night in the village of Upper Redding and a big crowd had gathered to enjoy the spectacular fireworks display.

High above them, someone else was watching, too.

"Ah! Home again!" said Ag the Alien, as he zoomed overhead in his brand new supercharged spaceship before he came in to land.

But Ag wasn't anywhere near his home. His planet was light years away across the galaxy. He was horribly lost and, worse still, he had no idea.

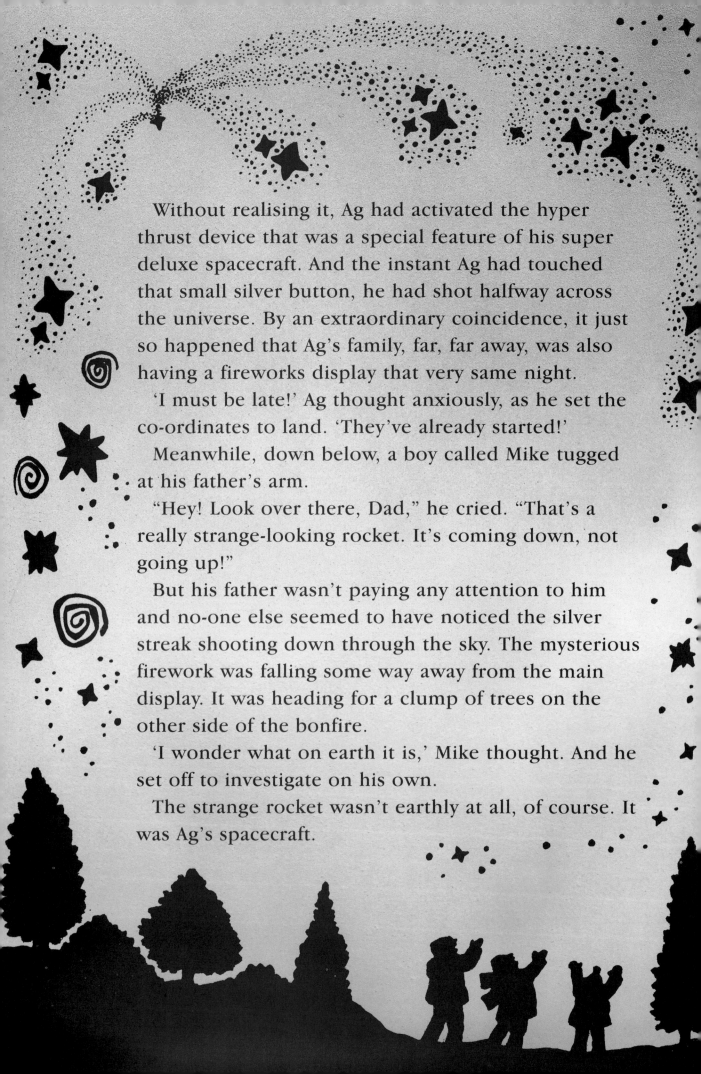

Without realising it, Ag had activated the hyper thrust device that was a special feature of his super deluxe spacecraft. And the instant Ag had touched that small silver button, he had shot halfway across the universe. By an extraordinary coincidence, it just so happened that Ag's family, far, far away, was also having a fireworks display that very same night.

'I must be late!' Ag thought anxiously, as he set the co-ordinates to land. 'They've already started!'

Meanwhile, down below, a boy called Mike tugged at his father's arm.

"Hey! Look over there, Dad," he cried. "That's a really strange-looking rocket. It's coming down, not going up!"

But his father wasn't paying any attention to him and no-one else seemed to have noticed the silver streak shooting down through the sky. The mysterious firework was falling some way away from the main display. It was heading for a clump of trees on the other side of the bonfire.

'I wonder what on earth it is,' Mike thought. And he set off to investigate on his own.

The strange rocket wasn't earthly at all, of course. It was Ag's spacecraft.

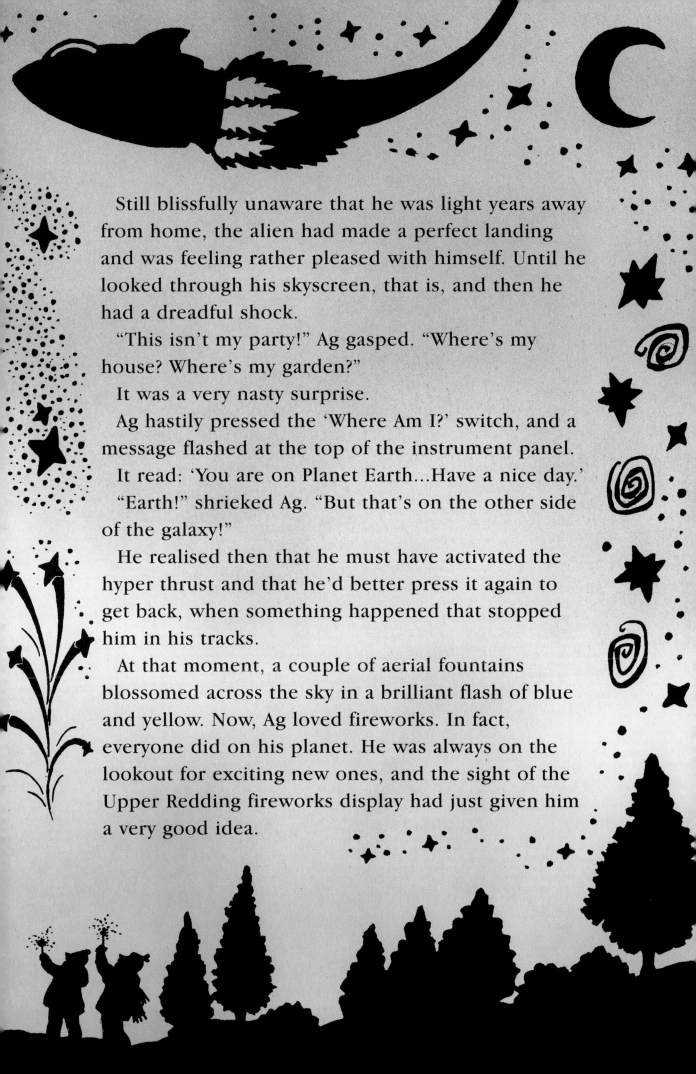

Still blissfully unaware that he was light years away from home, the alien had made a perfect landing and was feeling rather pleased with himself. Until he looked through his skyscreen, that is, and then he had a dreadful shock.

"This isn't my party!" Ag gasped. "Where's my house? Where's my garden?"

It was a very nasty surprise.

Ag hastily pressed the 'Where Am I?' switch, and a message flashed at the top of the instrument panel.

It read: 'You are on Planet Earth...Have a nice day.'

"Earth!" shrieked Ag. "But that's on the other side of the galaxy!"

He realised then that he must have activated the hyper thrust and that he'd better press it again to get back, when something happened that stopped him in his tracks.

At that moment, a couple of aerial fountains blossomed across the sky in a brilliant flash of blue and yellow. Now, Ag loved fireworks. In fact, everyone did on his planet. He was always on the lookout for exciting new ones, and the sight of the Upper Redding fireworks display had just given him a very good idea.

'Just think how thrilled everyone at home would be,' Ag thought, 'if I let off some fireworks that they had never ever seen before. I'd better just pop out and get some.'

So he armed himself with a laser gun, just in case it was not a friendly planet, jumped out of the spacecraft and hurried off in the direction of the Upper Redding bonfire.

Unfortunately, it was at exactly that moment that Mike arrived, hot on the trail of the strange rocket.

Bang! They ran straight into each other.

"Aagh!" yelled Mike at the sight of the alien.

"Do we know each other?" asked Ag, feeling very confused. "Pleased to meet you."

He had been about to blow the odd-looking creature to smithereens with his laser megablaster. But it seemed to recognise him. It had certainly said his name very enthusiastically.

Mike was also feeling very confused. But he saw the laser megablaster and quickly decided it would be wiser to make friends, as that was what the alien seemed to want to do.

"Er, pleased to meet you, too," he replied.

So they shook hands, or rather Ag shook a
hand and Mike shook a tentacle. It felt very odd
and rather squashy for both of them.

Mike was longing to ask Ag lots of questions,
like where he came from and what he was
doing. But the alien was in too much of a hurry.

"Now," said Ag. "You must take me to your
display. I need your fireworks immediately for
a party back home tonight."

Mike gulped. He couldn't think why an alien
would want fireworks and he was terrified of
what might happen if Ag appeared at the
bonfire. The sight of him would be enough to
send everyone running in every direction.
Even worse, the alien might be tempted to use
his laser megablaster on them. He had to
think of some way of ensuring that Ag got his
fireworks but somehow wasn't spotted.

"I'll get them for you," Mike replied hastily, wondering how he was going to remove any fireworks without anyone noticing, but realising he had no choice. "You can stay here."

Mike ran off. He was relieved to see that Ag had settled down to wait for his return, but what could he bring back? It would have to be something really good to satisfy the alien.

As he got nearer the bonfire, Mike got even more worried. But then he caught sight of something large, standing by itself, some way away from crowd and he realised he'd found the very thing. It was the grand finale to the display, a giant illuminated display that lit up in the shape of the village name, made out of multi-coloured catherine wheels. That would cause a sensation on an alien planet – but it was too heavy for him to lift!

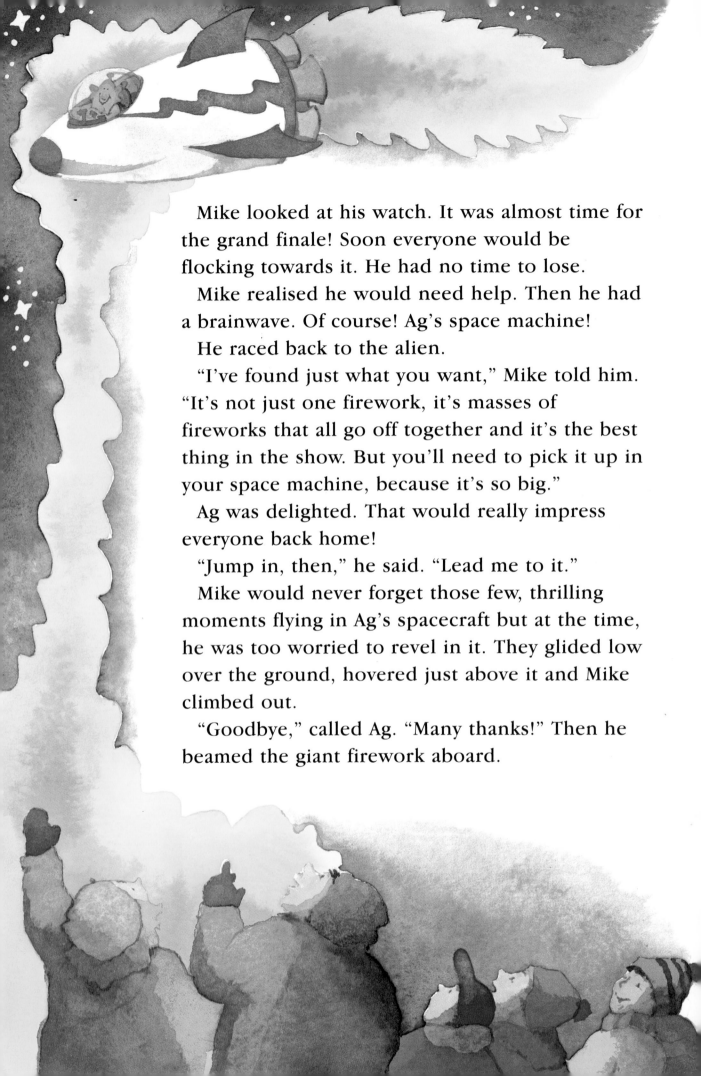

Mike looked at his watch. It was almost time for the grand finale! Soon everyone would be flocking towards it. He had no time to lose.

Mike realised he would need help. Then he had a brainwave. Of course! Ag's space machine!

He raced back to the alien.

"I've found just what you want," Mike told him. "It's not just one firework, it's masses of fireworks that all go off together and it's the best thing in the show. But you'll need to pick it up in your space machine, because it's so big."

Ag was delighted. That would really impress everyone back home!

"Jump in, then," he said. "Lead me to it."

Mike would never forget those few, thrilling moments flying in Ag's spacecraft but at the time, he was too worried to revel in it. They glided low over the ground, hovered just above it and Mike climbed out.

"Goodbye," called Ag. "Many thanks!" Then he beamed the giant firework aboard.

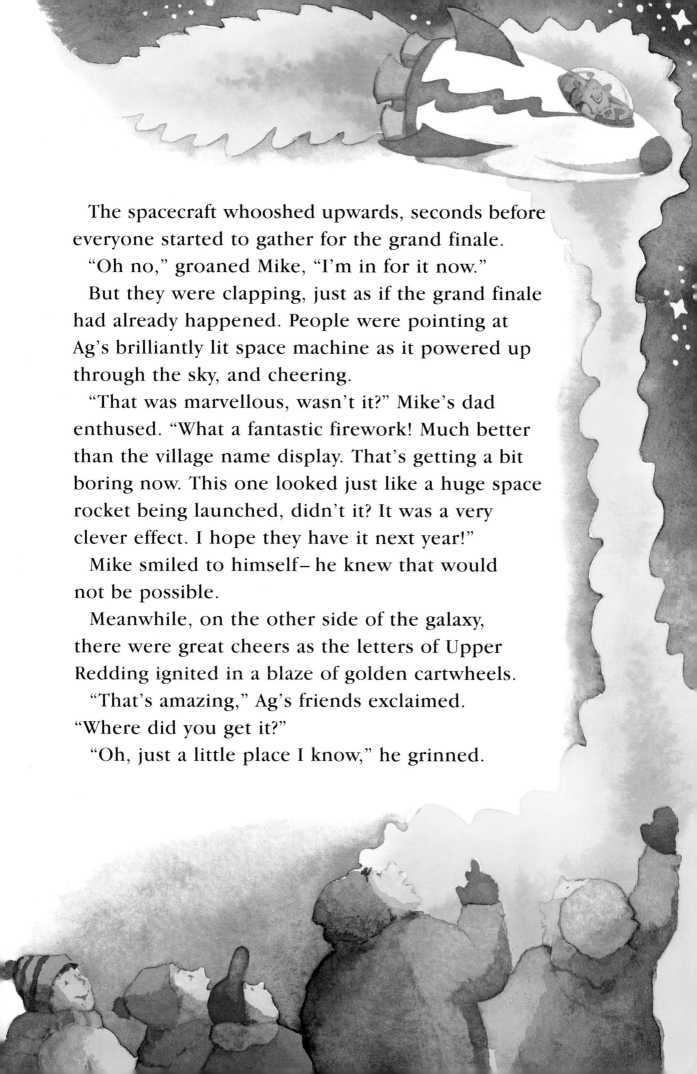

The spacecraft whooshed upwards, seconds before everyone started to gather for the grand finale.

"Oh no," groaned Mike, "I'm in for it now."

But they were clapping, just as if the grand finale had already happened. People were pointing at Ag's brilliantly lit space machine as it powered up through the sky, and cheering.

"That was marvellous, wasn't it?" Mike's dad enthused. "What a fantastic firework! Much better than the village name display. That's getting a bit boring now. This one looked just like a huge space rocket being launched, didn't it? It was a very clever effect. I hope they have it next year!"

Mike smiled to himself– he knew that would not be possible.

Meanwhile, on the other side of the galaxy, there were great cheers as the letters of Upper Redding ignited in a blaze of golden cartwheels.

"That's amazing," Ag's friends exclaimed. "Where did you get it?"

"Oh, just a little place I know," he grinned.

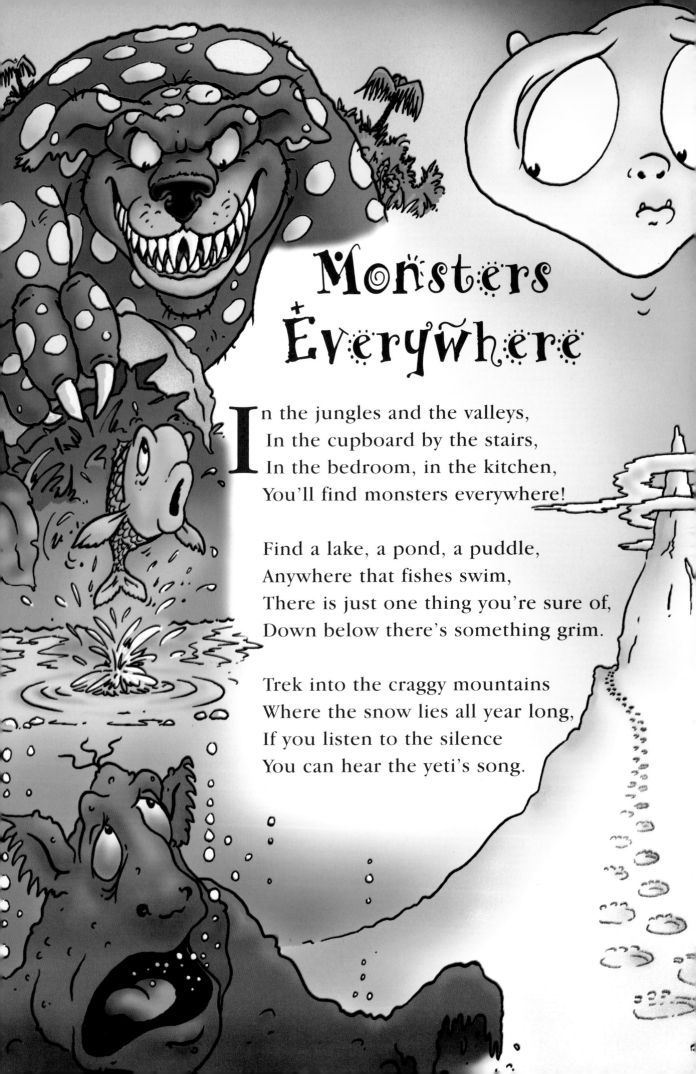

Monsters Everywhere

In the jungles and the valleys,
In the cupboard by the stairs,
In the bedroom, in the kitchen,
You'll find monsters everywhere!

Find a lake, a pond, a puddle,
Anywhere that fishes swim,
There is just one thing you're sure of,
Down below there's something grim.

Trek into the craggy mountains
Where the snow lies all year long,
If you listen to the silence
You can hear the yeti's song.

Gaze into the starry twilight,
You might glimpse a UFO,
Could it be from outer space?
You will never really know.

Steal a look inside a pyramid,
Just be careful when you do,
If you wake a sleeping mummy
He'll come clomping after you!

You might think it's just not safe
To go and visit anywhere,
As no one is ever sure
If the beasts are really there.

But they are imagination,
Not the same as telling lies,
We like to think there's more to life
Than can be seen through human eyes.

The Ogre's Hat

There once was an ogre, named Grindle, who lived alone in a rambling old house. Grindle had a terrible reputation, which he richly deserved, for being as nasty as possible and so no-one ever called to see him.

One day, when he was hunting for food in the woods, he spied a young woman. "Ah-ha!" said Grindle to himself. "A morsel to keep the hunger pangs at bay!" He pounced upon her and then he blinked and looked again. In his hairy fists he held, not a young woman, but a pedlar. "What....? How....?" growled Grindle in astonishment.

"Let me go and I'll explain," said the pedlar. Grindle reluctantly loosened his grasp and the pedlar said, "I have a magic hat. Every time I put it on, I change shape. I'm sure you won't like the taste of me, now I'm an old man!"

"You're still meat to me!" grumbled Grindle, grabbing the pedlar again.

"Wait!" cried the pedlar, fearing for his life. "Let me go and I'll give you my hat!" Grindle paused to scratch his grizzled chin. 'Well, it might be rather useful to go about in disguise,' he thought. "I'll take it!" he said, snatching the hat. It looked like a perfectly ordinary hat and he was about to protest that he had been swindled, when he realised that the pedlar had vanished.

Grindle carried the hat home. Once he was safely inside with the door firmly bolted, he couldn't resist trying it on. He stood in front of the mirror and carefully lowered the hat onto his filthy, tangled hair. He looked in the mirror and got the shock of his life. There stood a young prince in fine clothes with a crown on his head.

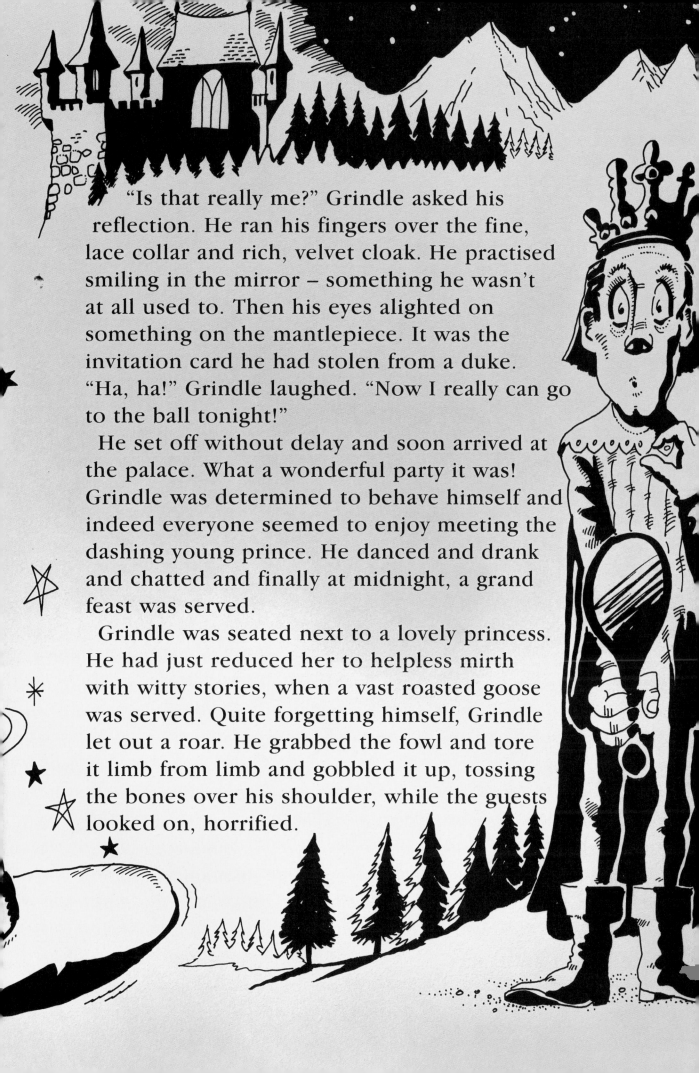

"Is that really me?" Grindle asked his reflection. He ran his fingers over the fine, lace collar and rich, velvet cloak. He practised smiling in the mirror – something he wasn't at all used to. Then his eyes alighted on something on the mantlepiece. It was the invitation card he had stolen from a duke. "Ha, ha!" Grindle laughed. "Now I really can go to the ball tonight!"

He set off without delay and soon arrived at the palace. What a wonderful party it was! Grindle was determined to behave himself and indeed everyone seemed to enjoy meeting the dashing young prince. He danced and drank and chatted and finally at midnight, a grand feast was served.

Grindle was seated next to a lovely princess. He had just reduced her to helpless mirth with witty stories, when a vast roasted goose was served. Quite forgetting himself, Grindle let out a roar. He grabbed the fowl and tore it limb from limb and gobbled it up, tossing the bones over his shoulder, while the guests looked on, horrified.

He stood up and looked around
wild-eyed. He was about to throttle the
princess, when the king shouted, "Arrest him!"
A pair of guards sprang forward, but Grindle
punched them flat as he charged towards the
door. "After him!" bellowed the king, but it was
too late. Grindle had bounded out into the
night and was away into the forest before
anyone could stop him.

The next morning, Grindle was mortified as
he remembered what had happened at the ball.
He pulled the sheets over his head, intending
to go back to sleep. But his eye was caught by
the crown on the mantlepiece. 'I'll put it on
and be a proper prince this time,' he thought.

Slowly, he lowered the crown onto his head.
To his great surprise, when he looked in the
mirror, he saw not a prince's crown, but a
chef's tall white hat and long white apron
'Well,' thought Grindle, 'it's about time I had a
proper job.' He set off for the town and soon
got a job in a bakery.

All day long, he mixed and stirred. He rolled
out pastry, he washed and wiped.

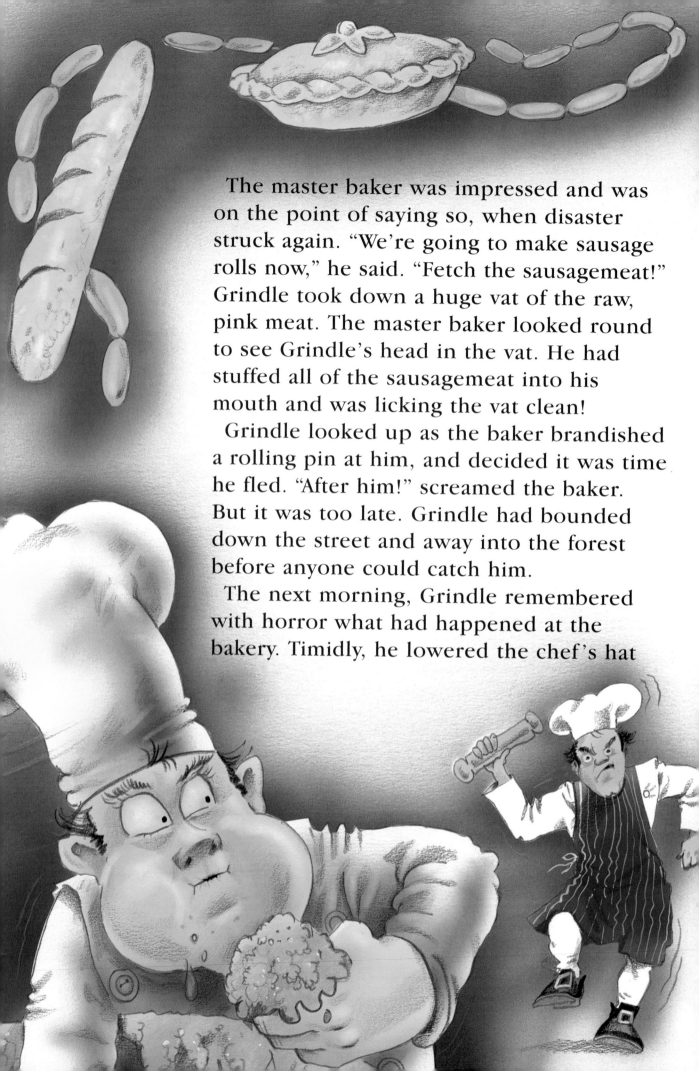

The master baker was impressed and was on the point of saying so, when disaster struck again. "We're going to make sausage rolls now," he said. "Fetch the sausagemeat!" Grindle took down a huge vat of the raw, pink meat. The master baker looked round to see Grindle's head in the vat. He had stuffed all of the sausagemeat into his mouth and was licking the vat clean!

Grindle looked up as the baker brandished a rolling pin at him, and decided it was time he fled. "After him!" screamed the baker. But it was too late. Grindle had bounded down the street and away into the forest before anyone could catch him.

The next morning, Grindle remembered with horror what had happened at the bakery. Timidly, he lowered the chef's hat

onto his head, fearful of what he might be turned into next. When he looked in the mirror, he saw that he had become a wizard, with a pointed hat, a flowing beard and a cape spangled with stars.

"Tee-hee!" cackled Grindle. "Now I'm going to have lots of fun being wicked and casting spells!" He pranced around the room, swishing his wand and brandishing a book called *Spells for Beginners*. Soon he was busy making a sign to hang on his front door. It said: 'Wizard Spell-Castings – Apply Within!' Grindle cracked his knuckles with glee. 'Who will be my first customer?' he wondered with excitement.

Just then, there was a knock.

Grindle threw the door wide open.

Who should be standing on the doorstep but the pedlar whose hat he had taken! Grindle tried to slam the door in his face, but the pedlar was too fast and pushed past him into the house.

'I know what to do!' thought Grindle. 'I'll just think of a spell. Now, let me see...' But, of course, he had never cast a spell before and without his book of spells in front of him he was lost.

"I've heard about your antics with my hat," scolded the pedlar. "I'm taking it back. Apologise for what you've done, or I'll tell the king who ruined his feast!"

So Grindle said how very sorry he was. Then he told the pedlar how unhappy he was alone in his great mansion.

The pedlar was really a kindly soul and took pity on him.

"I have another hat for you," he said. "With this one you'll never be unhappy again." He handed Grindle a battered old straw hat and was gone.

Grindle was bemused. Cautiously, he put the hat on and looked in the mirror. He looked the same as ever, but he felt totally different! He wanted to make music, so he found his tin whistle and started to play. He had never felt so happy in his life; he danced into the town, and headed for the market square. There he set the old hat out on the cobbles for people's coins and played and danced for joy the whole day long. And he was never unhappy again.

A Monster in the Garden

"Hooray," shouted Dad, waving the letter in his hand. "That's terrific. It's the best news I've ever heard. It's from the people who are building the new motorway. They're going to give us lots of money for the house. Now we can buy that other one we've been looking at."

The motorway was coming. Nothing could stop it now. It was going to come straight through our house, across the fields and woods at the back and close to the hill, where the caves were. It made me sad. I liked our house. I didn't want them to knock it down so that they could build a noisy, smelly motorway.

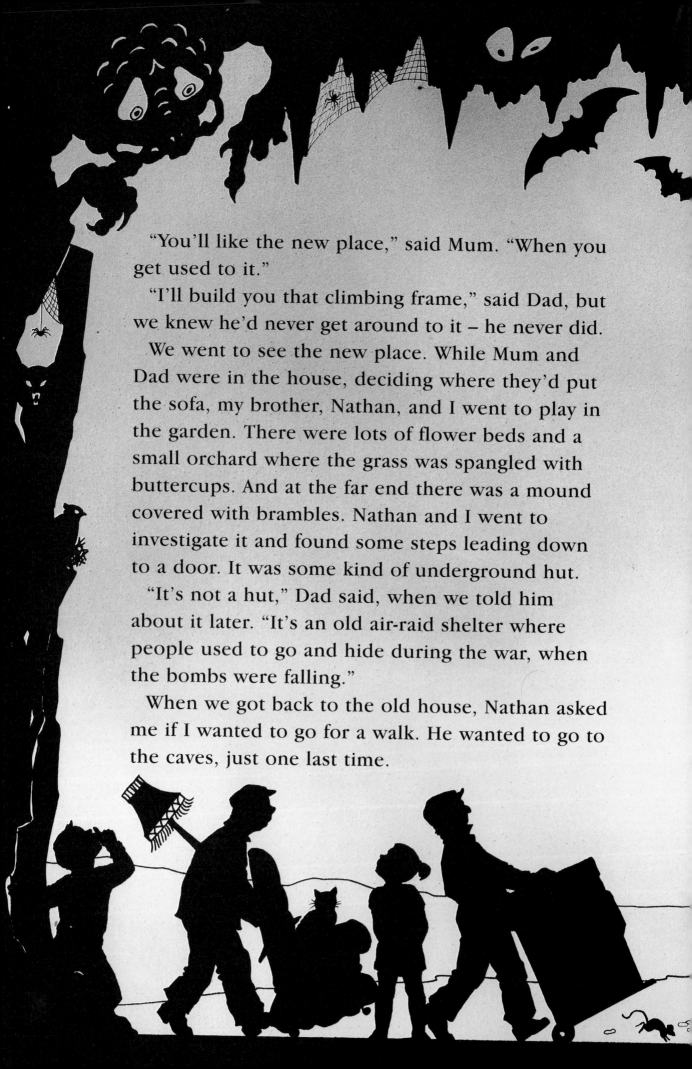

"You'll like the new place," said Mum. "When you get used to it."

"I'll build you that climbing frame," said Dad, but we knew he'd never get around to it – he never did.

We went to see the new place. While Mum and Dad were in the house, deciding where they'd put the sofa, my brother, Nathan, and I went to play in the garden. There were lots of flower beds and a small orchard where the grass was spangled with buttercups. And at the far end there was a mound covered with brambles. Nathan and I went to investigate it and found some steps leading down to a door. It was some kind of underground hut.

"It's not a hut," Dad said, when we told him about it later. "It's an old air-raid shelter where people used to go and hide during the war, when the bombs were falling."

When we got back to the old house, Nathan asked me if I wanted to go for a walk. He wanted to go to the caves, just one last time.

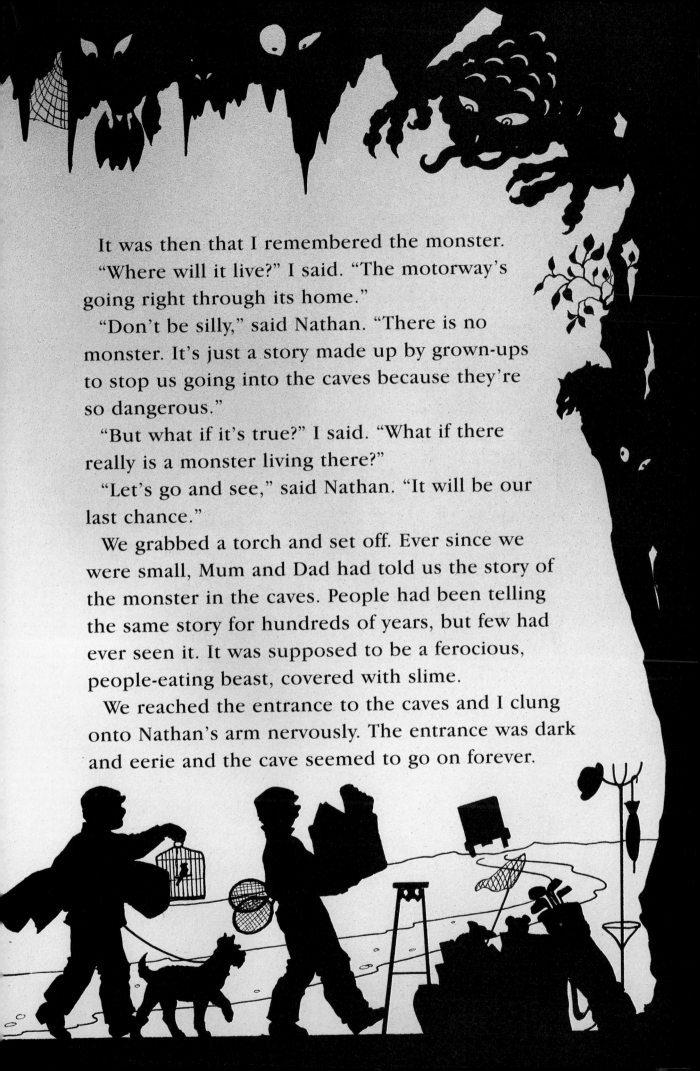

It was then that I remembered the monster.

"Where will it live?" I said. "The motorway's going right through its home."

"Don't be silly," said Nathan. "There is no monster. It's just a story made up by grown-ups to stop us going into the caves because they're so dangerous."

"But what if it's true?" I said. "What if there really is a monster living there?"

"Let's go and see," said Nathan. "It will be our last chance."

We grabbed a torch and set off. Ever since we were small, Mum and Dad had told us the story of the monster in the caves. People had been telling the same story for hundreds of years, but few had ever seen it. It was supposed to be a ferocious, people-eating beast, covered with slime.

We reached the entrance to the caves and I clung onto Nathan's arm nervously. The entrance was dark and eerie and the cave seemed to go on forever.

We walked slowly inside, and soon we were in complete darkness. Nathan switched on the torch and the beam showed a series of caves going deeper and deeper into the hill. It was cold and damp. We could feel the water dripping down from above. Suddenly I heard a noise. A strange, slurping noise.

"Don't move," Nathan whispered. "I'm sure that there's something in here."

He swung the beam to the left and right and there it was, crouching at the back of the cave, staring at us with large, dark eyes. It was quite big, about the size of a fridge. Its skin was covered with bumps and warts and its mouth was wide and dribbling. It looked just like a giant frog. When the torch beam lit up its face, the monster grunted and shaded its eyes. But it didn't move.

"Hello," said Nathan (he really can be very stupid sometimes). But the monster just grunted as if to say hello back.

"I wish we had some food for it," whispered Nathan. "That way it would know that we were friendly. I wonder what it eats?"

"Us, probably," I gulped.

"No, I think it would have gone for us by now, if it was going to," he said. He slowly stepped closer.

"It's all right," he said. "I think it's harmless." Nathan and the monster studied each other. Then Nathan said, slowly and clearly, "We came to warn you that there's a new motorway coming. It's going to come right through here. You're not safe here. You need to find a new, safe place to live." The monster opened its big, orange, watery eyes wide and looked terrified.

"Don't worry," said Nathan. "We'll think of something." The monster grunted, sounding

relieved and Nathan came back to where I was standing. Then we ran home.

"Oh, the poor monster," I said. "What shall we do?"

"We'll have to think of somewhere new for it to live," said Nathan. Then he suddenly stopped and grabbed my arm. "I know," he said. "The air-raid shelter in the new garden. It's perfect. It's the closest thing to a cave we'll ever find."

It was a great idea, but how were we going to get the monster to the new place without being seen? It was too far to walk.

A week passed, and Mum and Dad packed everything into cases, ready for the move. Then the removal vans arrived. Two whole vans just for us. When everything was loaded, the driver said, "Is that it?"

"Yes, that's the lot," replied Dad.

"Are you sure?" said the driver. "Because there's a space in the second van the size of a big fridge. It would be a shame not to use it and then find later that you've forgotten something."

I looked at Nathan, and he looked at me.

"Let's have lunch," said Mum, "and then we'll get moving."

While they were eating, Nathan and I ran back to the caves. The monster was where we'd left it.

"We've found you a new home," said Nathan. "Come with us."

The monster grunted and followed us out of the cave. It moved in an odd half-walking, half-hopping way with a slightly unpleasant slurping noise, but it could move quite quickly.

No-one was around. We opened the van and the monster jumped up into the space that was left and blinked at us trustingly. When we got to the new house, the van drivers went inside to see where Mum and Dad wanted everything.

Quick as a flash, we opened the door of the van and the monster fell out onto the road with a loud plop. After a quick check that no-one was about, we ran down the garden to the air-raid shelter. The door opened with a grating noise. The monster looked inside the dark, damp interior and made a happy squeaking sound and then disappeared inside.

Two days later, just as he was going to work, Dad cornered Nathan and me in the hallway.

"Now, I don't want you two going anywhere near that air-raid shelter," he said. "Do you understand? It's dangerous."

"We won't Dad," I said, and then I shivered. "It looks like the sort of place where a big monster might live, and I bet it could eat us up in one gulp."

Dad ruffled my hair. "That's right," he laughed. "I'll pull it all down one day. When I get around to it."

But we knew he wouldn't – well not for ages.

When Monsters Go To Fancy Dress Parties

When there's a fancy dress party
You can be just who you please,
A pirate, a king or a princess,
Or a monster can be a good wheeze.

As a monster you can be awful,
Make a loud noise and be rude,
Scare everybody by pulling a face,
And roar when you want some mor food.

But what is it like for real monsters
When asked to a fancy dress do?
Do they dress up in a costume
And go as a person like you?

Do they put on their best outfits
And think of polite things to say?
Nibble no more than a modest amount
And dance in a fashionable way?

Monsters aren't good at pretending
They gulp down their food in one go,
When they take to the floor for a tango
They jerk and they stamp to and fro.

They all hate to play pass the parcel,
Their clothes get so covered with grime,
They cannot play musical statues,
They simply slip up in the slime.

No, monsters will always be monstrous,
It's a fact that you just cannot hide,
You might make a monster look human,
But you can't change the monster inside.

Dodging the Dragon

"**R**rroar!"

Jill stepped back quickly and trod on her brother's foot.

"What is it?" she gasped, looking up at a giant, spiky dinosaur guarding the entrance to the Monster Games Fair.

"Ouch! Mind my new trainers," said James crossly. He looked up, too. "Don't be so silly! It's just pretend."

The dinosaur roared again. Jill listened hard. It did sound a bit metallic but it was still a pretty scary noise and the huge model was very lifelike. 'If this was just the start of the fair,' she thought, 'what was the rest of it going to be like?'

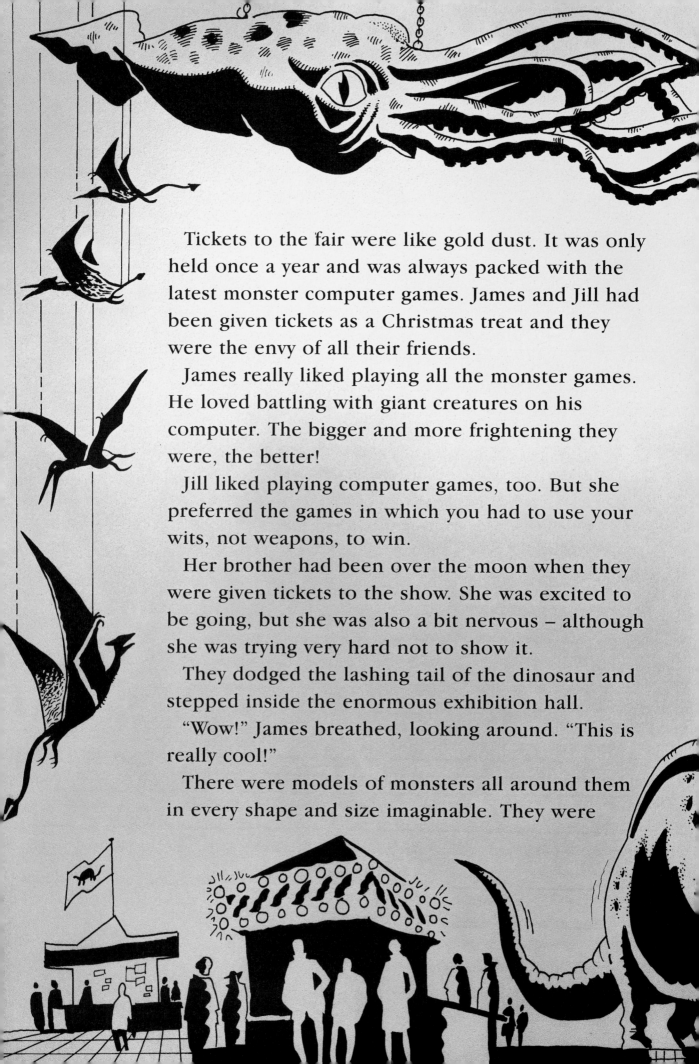

Tickets to the fair were like gold dust. It was only held once a year and was always packed with the latest monster computer games. James and Jill had been given tickets as a Christmas treat and they were the envy of all their friends.

James really liked playing all the monster games. He loved battling with giant creatures on his computer. The bigger and more frightening they were, the better!

Jill liked playing computer games, too. But she preferred the games in which you had to use your wits, not weapons, to win.

Her brother had been over the moon when they were given tickets to the show. She was excited to be going, but she was also a bit nervous – although she was trying very hard not to show it.

They dodged the lashing tail of the dinosaur and stepped inside the enormous exhibition hall.

"Wow!" James breathed, looking around. "This is really cool!"

There were models of monsters all around them in every shape and size imaginable. They were

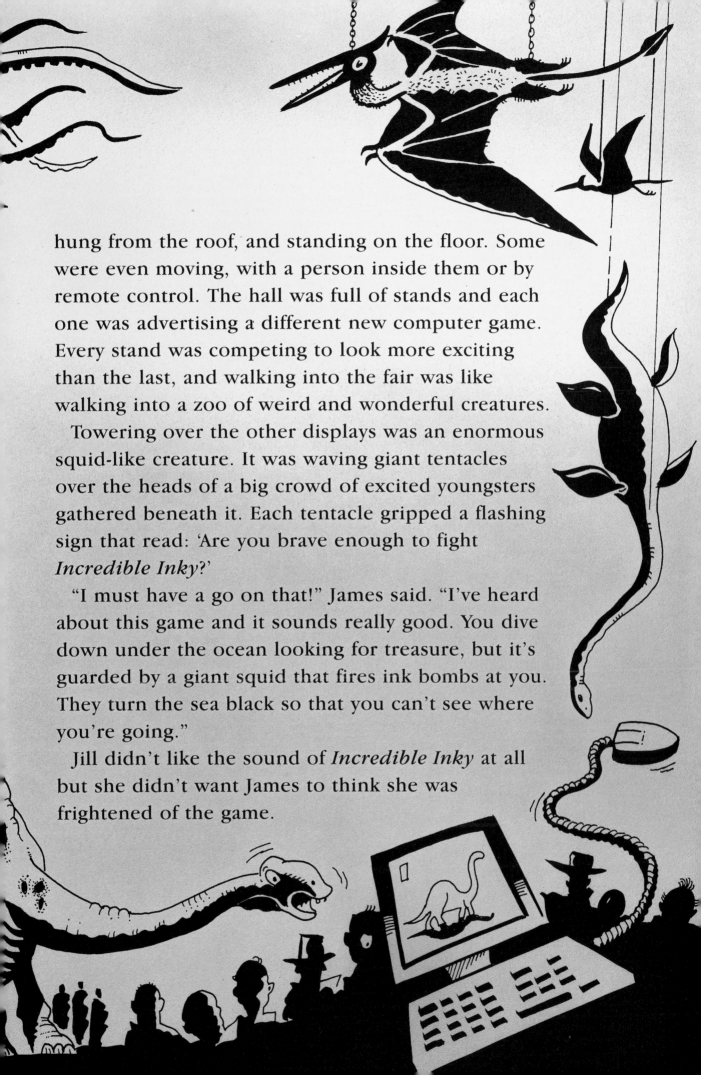

hung from the roof, and standing on the floor. Some were even moving, with a person inside them or by remote control. The hall was full of stands and each one was advertising a different new computer game. Every stand was competing to look more exciting than the last, and walking into the fair was like walking into a zoo of weird and wonderful creatures.

Towering over the other displays was an enormous squid-like creature. It was waving giant tentacles over the heads of a big crowd of excited youngsters gathered beneath it. Each tentacle gripped a flashing sign that read: 'Are you brave enough to fight *Incredible Inky*?'

"I must have a go on that!" James said. "I've heard about this game and it sounds really good. You dive down under the ocean looking for treasure, but it's guarded by a giant squid that fires ink bombs at you. They turn the sea black so that you can't see where you're going."

Jill didn't like the sound of *Incredible Inky* at all but she didn't want James to think she was frightened of the game.

"Let's split up," she told her brother. "I want to look at everything first before I have a go at any of the games. We can meet at the entrance again in an hour's time."

James looked at his sister in disgust.

"You're just scared!" he scoffed. "See you in an hour – if you haven't fainted by then," he added scornfully.

James ran off to join the queue to play *Incredible Inky*.

Jill took a deep breath. Her brother could be so mean! Well, she'd show him.

"I'm not scared!" she shouted after him, but he was out of earshot.

There was a tap on her shoulder. A large, fearsome-looking green monster stood beside her.

"I heard what you just said," the man inside the monster said. "I need someone who's not scared to play our new *Dodging the Dragon* game. Follow me."

"Okay," Jill replied. She was still so angry with James, just at that moment she felt brave enough to fight off ten dragons.

The monster led Jill to a platform with a big screen raised above the rest of the hall.

There were people sitting in rows of chairs around it.

They seemed to be waiting for something to happen.

The monster took Jill's hand in its large paw and they climbed up some steps and onto the platform, where a man dressed a bit like a circus ringmaster was waiting.

As soon as he saw Jill with the dragon, he smiled at her, and asked her what her name was and then grabbed a microphone.

"Let's give a big hand to a brave little lady," the man announced. "This is Jill and she's going to play *Dodging the Dragon*!"

'Oh no!' thought Jill. 'I'm going to be put on show!'

The man sat Jill down at a computer which had been set up on the stage beside the massive screen.

"You'll be playing the game on this computer," he told her. "But it will also appear on the large screen so that your audience can enjoy the action, too. Good luck!"

Jill took a deep breath. She tried not to think of all the people watching and waited for the game to appear on the computer screen.

The snapping jaws of a dragon suddenly filled the screen and a jet of fire issued from its cavernous mouth. She gasped and there was a murmur of excitement from the audience… the game had begun!

The screen changed. The dragon had gone and she was walking through an empty house. A bat flew low overhead. Jill ducked and so did some of the audience. It was all so real!

Some words flashed across the screen. 'You are in the deserted house,' Jill read. 'But it is not deserted. A dragon guards the only exit. To win the game you must dodge the dragon and escape through it.'

Jill walked down a corridor which then split into two. Which way should she go?

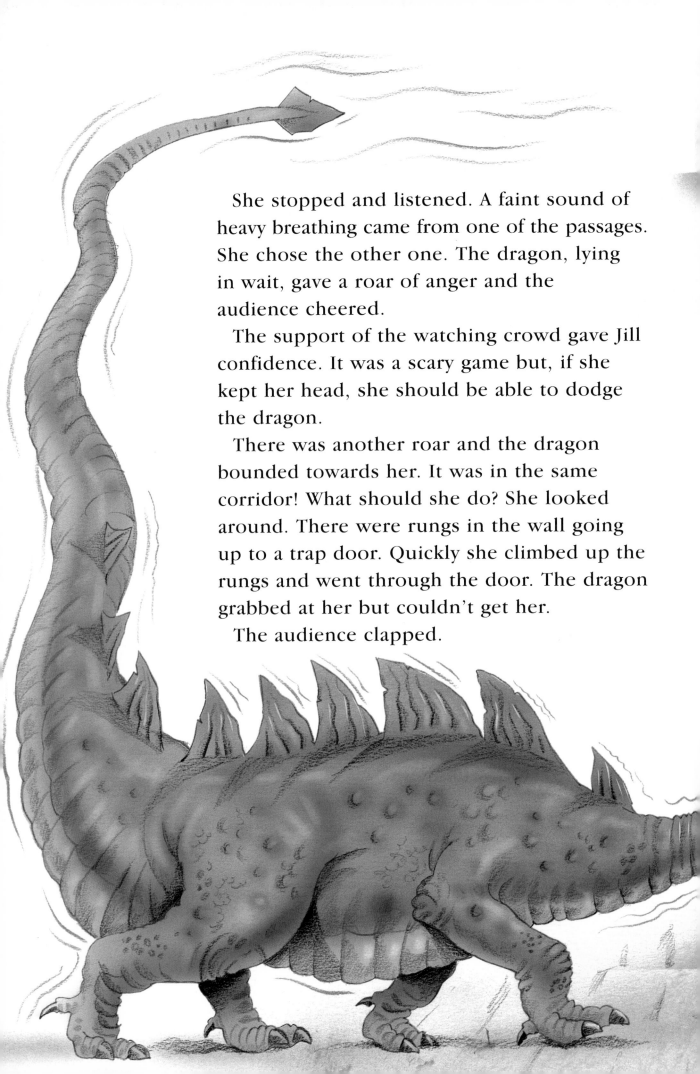

She stopped and listened. A faint sound of heavy breathing came from one of the passages. She chose the other one. The dragon, lying in wait, gave a roar of anger and the audience cheered.

The support of the watching crowd gave Jill confidence. It was a scary game but, if she kept her head, she should be able to dodge the dragon.

There was another roar and the dragon bounded towards her. It was in the same corridor! What should she do? She looked around. There were rungs in the wall going up to a trap door. Quickly she climbed up the rungs and went through the door. The dragon grabbed at her but couldn't get her.

The audience clapped.

Jill was now in an attic. Through
the thick cobwebs, she could see a
door. Would the dragon be behind it?
She held her breath and opened it.

There was no monster and she was
standing at the top of what looked like
a fire escape.

'What a stroke of luck!' she thought
excitedly. 'This must be the way out!'

The ground was a long way below her
and the fire escape was full of twists and
turns. She was only half way down, when
there was another roar. The dragon burst
out of the attic door and started to run
down behind her, shooting out jets of fire.

Someone in the audience tried to cover
a scream.

Jill dodged the flames but realised the dragon would soon overtake her. It was coming down so fast. Then she spotted a rope. It was tied to the railings and hung down to the ground. She leapt onto it and slid down, landing safely on the grass outside the house. The dragon gave a final, ear-splitting roar. It vanished and the screen went blank again.

"Congratulations, Jill!" the man in charge said. "You dodged the dragon in record time. We'd like to present you with this trophy."

He presented Jill with a silver cup decorated with dragons, as the audience clapped and cheered.

"Well done!" said an admiring voice.

It was James. "You were the star of the fair's main event. I was watching it all and you put on a really good show. That was a terrifying dragon but you weren't at all frightened!"

"Oh, were you scared?" Jill smiled. "I wasn't a bit!"

And the funny thing was, Jill realised, she wasn't pretending any more. After her battle with the dragon, she really meant it.

The Timid Troll

Timothy the Timid Troll
Though horrible and hairy,
Had a meek, mild mannered streak
That simply wasn't scary.

Whilst other Trolls could terrify
With gruff and grotesque growls,
Timothy was far behind
Still practising his scowls.

His mother took him to one side
And peering down her glasses,
She asked him why he was so shy
And hopeless at his classes.

Her son replied, all misty eyed,
"I'd like to learn to sing."
His father said, "Don't be absurd,
Who's heard of such a thing?"

His parents gave the boy his way
Though this was not their choice.
A horrid son would be more fun
Than one with a splendid voice.

Although Tim tried with all his might
The highest notes to reach,
All that he could manage was
A shrill and evil screech.

A sound that froze the very soul
And made the windows crack.
"That's our lad," said Mum to Dad
And slapped him on the back.

The Monster's Hill

Just outside Farsham there's an unusual hill. It has very steep sides and rises to sharp peak. You can see it from a long way off. In the summer, families enjoy picnics there, and in the winter snow the children of Farsham toboggan down it at great speeds. You can hear them whooping and yelling with joy.

After one such cold and exciting morning, Mary visited her grandfather.

"Did you have fun on the Monster's Hill?" he asked her.

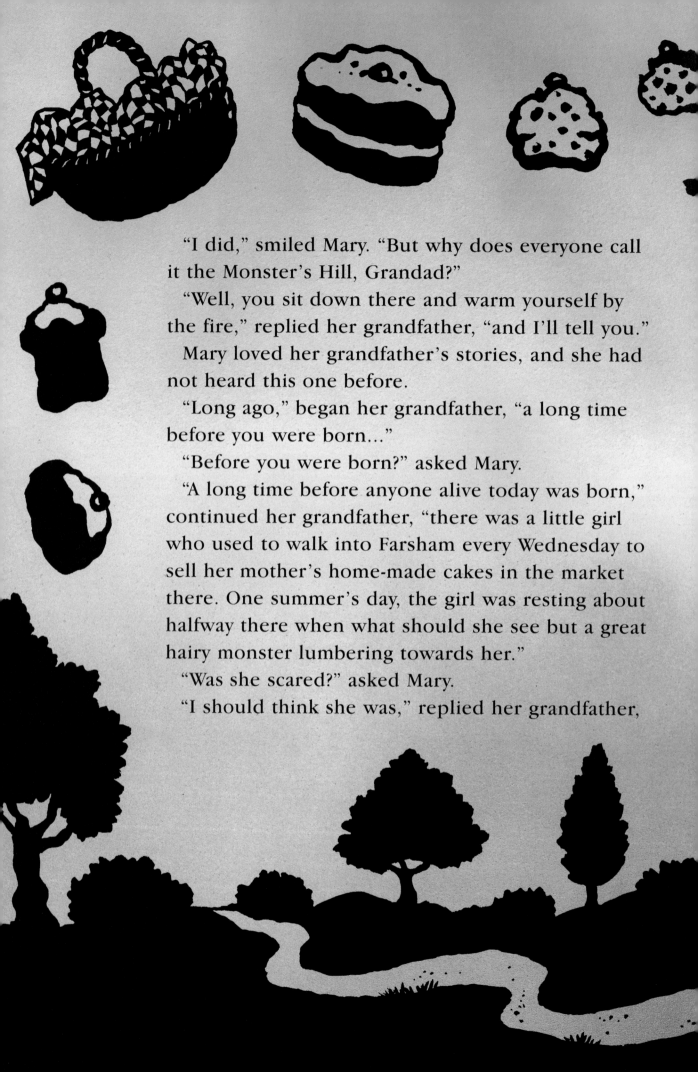

"I did," smiled Mary. "But why does everyone call it the Monster's Hill, Grandad?"

"Well, you sit down there and warm yourself by the fire," replied her grandfather, "and I'll tell you."

Mary loved her grandfather's stories, and she had not heard this one before.

"Long ago," began her grandfather, "a long time before you were born..."

"Before you were born?" asked Mary.

"A long time before anyone alive today was born," continued her grandfather, "there was a little girl who used to walk into Farsham every Wednesday to sell her mother's home-made cakes in the market there. One summer's day, the girl was resting about halfway there when what should she see but a great hairy monster lumbering towards her."

"Was she scared?" asked Mary.

"I should think she was," replied her grandfather,

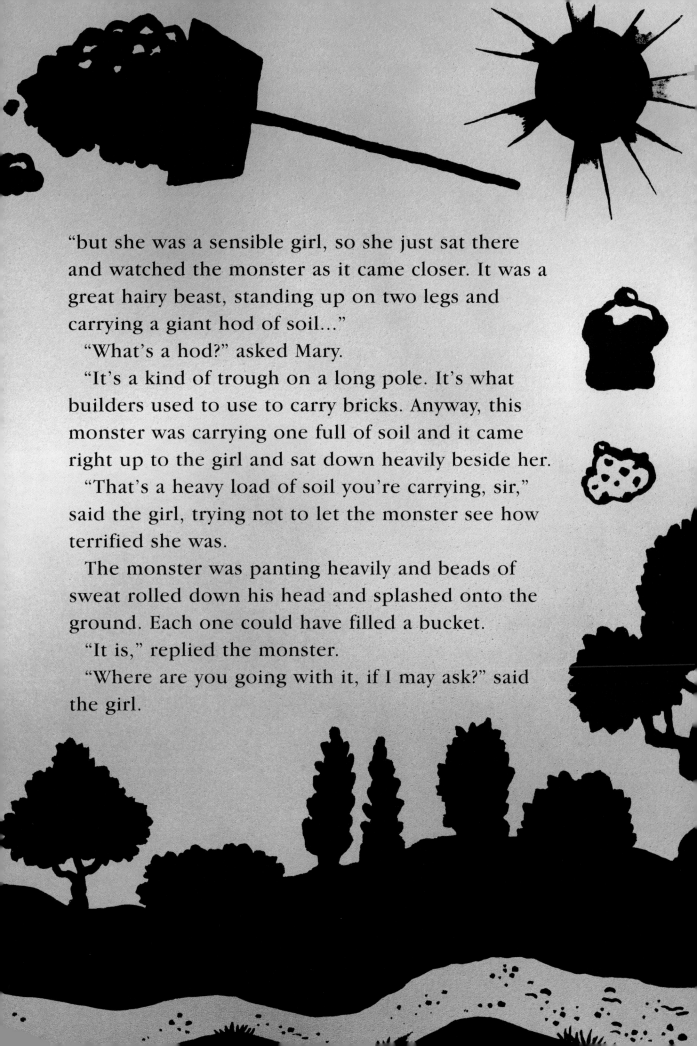

"but she was a sensible girl, so she just sat there and watched the monster as it came closer. It was a great hairy beast, standing up on two legs and carrying a giant hod of soil..."

"What's a hod?" asked Mary.

"It's a kind of trough on a long pole. It's what builders used to use to carry bricks. Anyway, this monster was carrying one full of soil and it came right up to the girl and sat down heavily beside her.

"That's a heavy load of soil you're carrying, sir," said the girl, trying not to let the monster see how terrified she was.

The monster was panting heavily and beads of sweat rolled down his head and splashed onto the ground. Each one could have filled a bucket.

"It is," replied the monster.

"Where are you going with it, if I may ask?" said the girl.

"To Farsham, little girl."

That's where the girl was heading with her cakes, but she didn't think a great big hairy monster with a hod full of soil could possibly be up to any good, so she didn't say so.

"And what are you going to do when you get there?" she asked politely.

The monster turned to her with a laugh.

"I'm going to dump it in the path of the river, so that the water flows around it and right into the city. Then all the people there, and especially the mayor, will drown and their houses will be swept away."

"Do you dislike the people of Farsham that much?" asked the girl, trying not to show her dislike of the monster and his wicked plan.

"Not so much the people, but the mayor especially," said the monster. "He has been rude to me, and I am going to teach him a lesson."

Now, the little girl did not know the Mayor of Farsham, but she didn't want the people of the city to be drowned. If they were swept away, who would buy her mother's cakes?

"The thing is," continued the monster, "I don't know where Farsham is. I've been walking around all morning and I can't find it. Do you know where it is?"

The girl thought for a moment and then said, "Yes, sir. I know where it is. In fact I'm going there myself today to sell these cakes. I'll show you the way if you like."

"That would be most kind," said the monster. "Lead the way."

The girl, now fully rested, stood up and set off. The monster lifted his hod to his shoulder and followed her. But the girl did not head straight for Farsham as she would

normally have done; she set off in another direction, towards the Munton Hills. The sun rose high in the sky and was soon very hot. The girl strode on across fields of wheat and barley, and through meadows high with grass. The monster trod slowly behind her, his feet thump, thump, thumping along the ground, and he grew weary, very weary. His hod was heavy and he wasn't used to walking so far.

"Are you sure this is the way to Farsham?" the monster said grumpily, after an hour.

"Oh, this is the way," the girl assured him. "But we still have a long way to go."

They tramped over the Munton Hills and on across the countryside. Another hour passed and another, and the monster grew wearier and wearier and hotter and hotter, and still there was no sign of Farsham.

The girl was tired too. Her basket of cakes was not light and she had already been up since dawn. Her shoes were nearly worn through. But she didn't show it. She kept right on walking, and at last the monster said, with a heavy sigh, "Stop. This is hopeless. This hod is too heavy and I'm too hot. I can't go on. I'm as tired as a mountain. I'm going to leave this soil here and go home. I've had enough."

And with that, the monster upturned his hod and dumped his soil right there where he had been sitting. And that great pile of soil is what we call The Monster's Hill to this very day.

"But it's not far from Farsham," said Mary.

"Yes, he was close," replied her grandfather. "If he hadn't listened to the girl and had gone on another half an hour or so, he would have made it to the city and drowned everyone. But the girl saved them."

"What did she do next?' asked Mary.

"She stumbled into the city, with her feet sore

and blistered and her shoes worn through and went straight to the Mayor and told him what had happened."

"Did he believe her?"

"When he saw the great pile of soil he did," said her grandfather. "He had a new pair of shoes made for the girl and declared that that day should be a holiday every year, in celebration and thanks for the girl whose cunning and bravery had saved the city."

"That's the 22 July?"

"That's right," said her grandfather. "The day when everyone has a holiday, except the shoe-shops, and they all buy a new pair of shoes and walk out to The Monster's Hill."

The following summer, Mary and her grandfather met in the Square on 22 July and together they walked to The Monster's Hill. Everyone was there.

'But,' thought Mary, 'I wonder how many of them know why...'

The School Monster

Some schools have a cat, a fluffy rabbit or a pair of fish. St Stephen's School was very different – it had a pet monster. Mortimer Monster, as he was known, was as big as the bike shed but luckily he didn't live in it. In the winter he liked to wrap himself around the boiler house because it was lovely and warm. In the summer he sunned himself by the pool and let the schoolchildren use his tail as a waterslide.

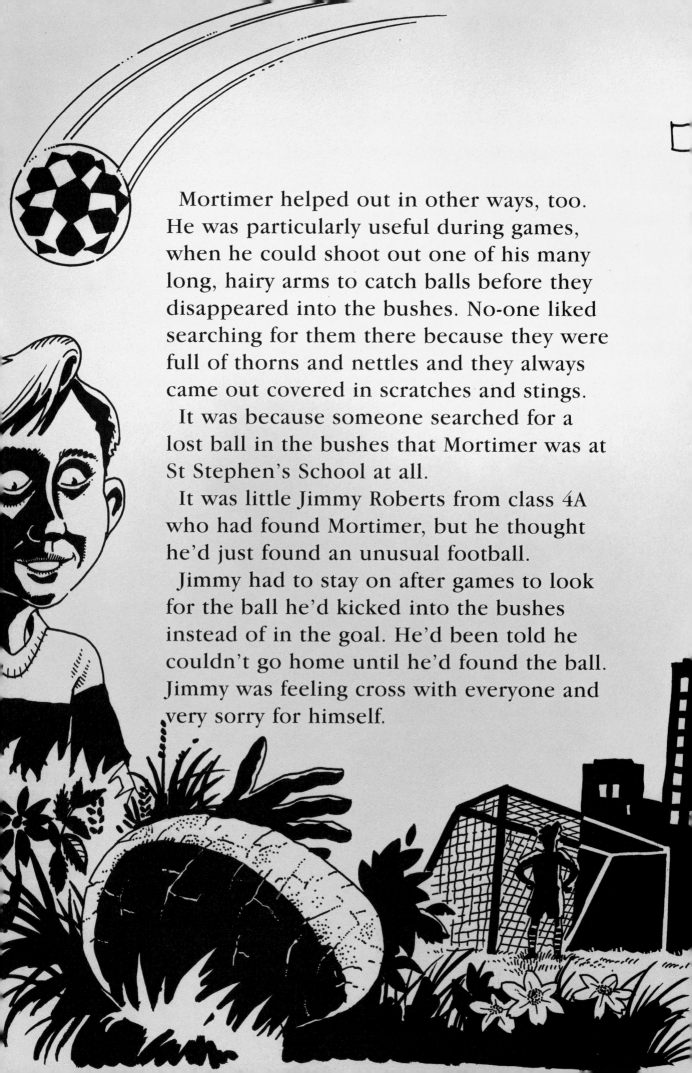

Mortimer helped out in other ways, too. He was particularly useful during games, when he could shoot out one of his many long, hairy arms to catch balls before they disappeared into the bushes. No-one liked searching for them there because they were full of thorns and nettles and they always came out covered in scratches and stings.

It was because someone searched for a lost ball in the bushes that Mortimer was at St Stephen's School at all.

It was little Jimmy Roberts from class 4A who had found Mortimer, but he thought he'd just found an unusual football.

Jimmy had to stay on after games to look for the ball he'd kicked into the bushes instead of in the goal. He'd been told he couldn't go home until he'd found the ball. Jimmy was feeling cross with everyone and very sorry for himself.

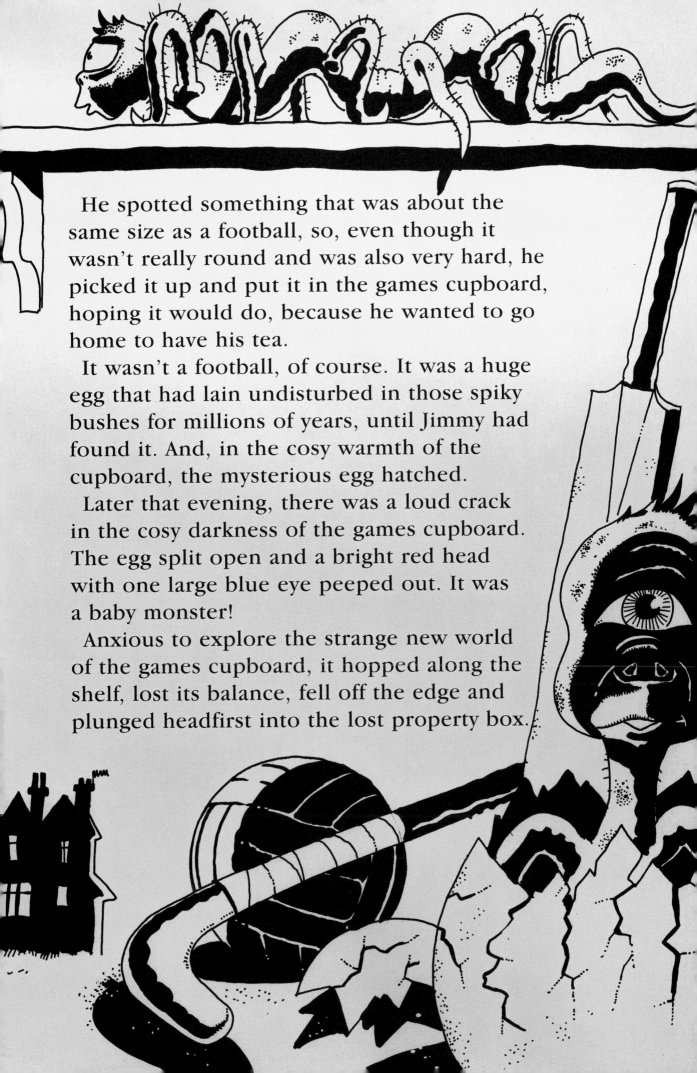

He spotted something that was about the same size as a football, so, even though it wasn't really round and was also very hard, he picked it up and put it in the games cupboard, hoping it would do, because he wanted to go home to have his tea.

It wasn't a football, of course. It was a huge egg that had lain undisturbed in those spiky bushes for millions of years, until Jimmy had found it. And, in the cosy warmth of the cupboard, the mysterious egg hatched.

Later that evening, there was a loud crack in the cosy darkness of the games cupboard. The egg split open and a bright red head with one large blue eye peeped out. It was a baby monster!

Anxious to explore the strange new world of the games cupboard, it hopped along the shelf, lost its balance, fell off the edge and plunged headfirst into the lost property box.

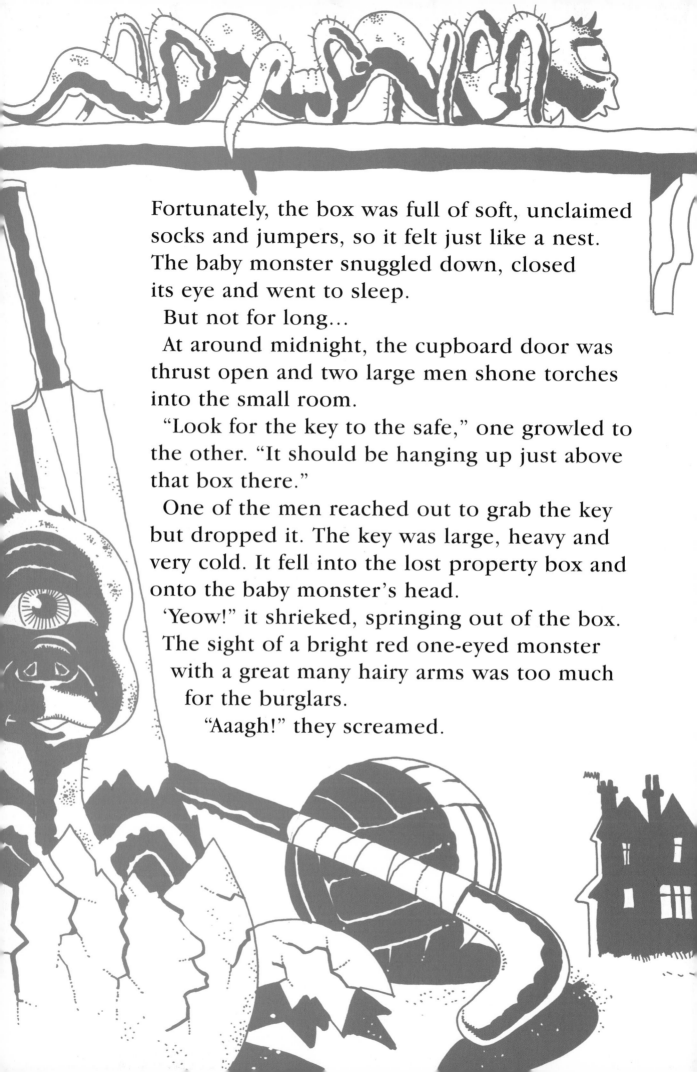

Fortunately, the box was full of soft, unclaimed socks and jumpers, so it felt just like a nest. The baby monster snuggled down, closed its eye and went to sleep.

But not for long…

At around midnight, the cupboard door was thrust open and two large men shone torches into the small room.

"Look for the key to the safe," one growled to the other. "It should be hanging up just above that box there."

One of the men reached out to grab the key but dropped it. The key was large, heavy and very cold. It fell into the lost property box and onto the baby monster's head.

'Yeow!" it shrieked, springing out of the box. The sight of a bright red one-eyed monster with a great many hairy arms was too much for the burglars.

"Aaagh!" they screamed.

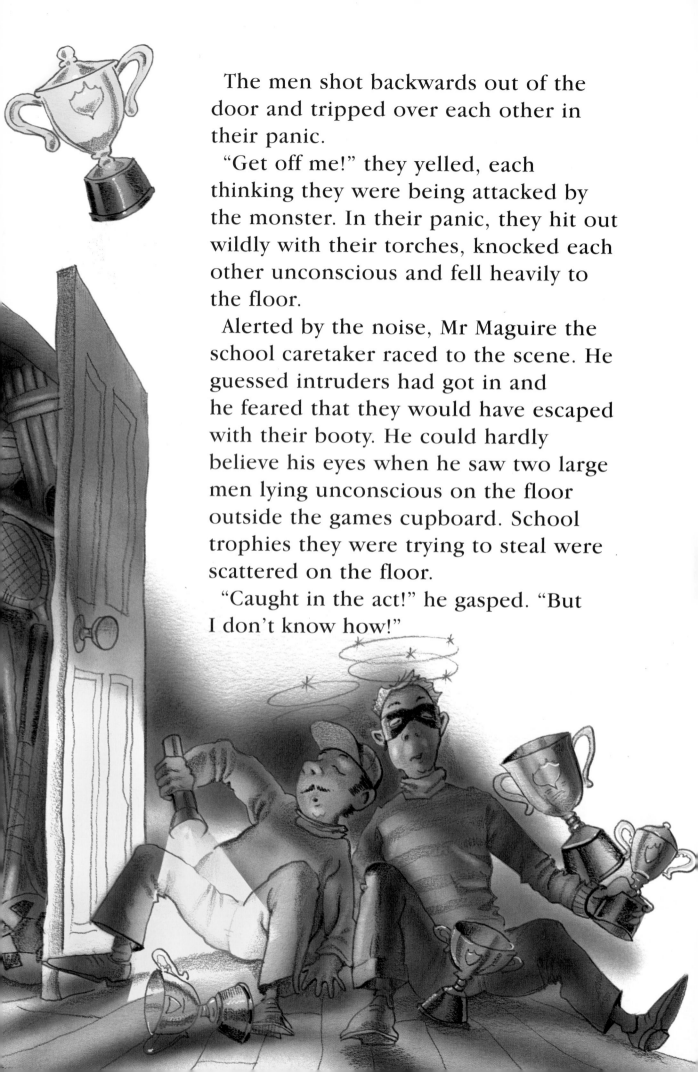

The men shot backwards out of the door and tripped over each other in their panic.

"Get off me!" they yelled, each thinking they were being attacked by the monster. In their panic, they hit out wildly with their torches, knocked each other unconscious and fell heavily to the floor.

Alerted by the noise, Mr Maguire the school caretaker raced to the scene. He guessed intruders had got in and he feared that they would have escaped with their booty. He could hardly believe his eyes when he saw two large men lying unconscious on the floor outside the games cupboard. School trophies they were trying to steal were scattered on the floor.

"Caught in the act!" he gasped. "But I don't know how!"

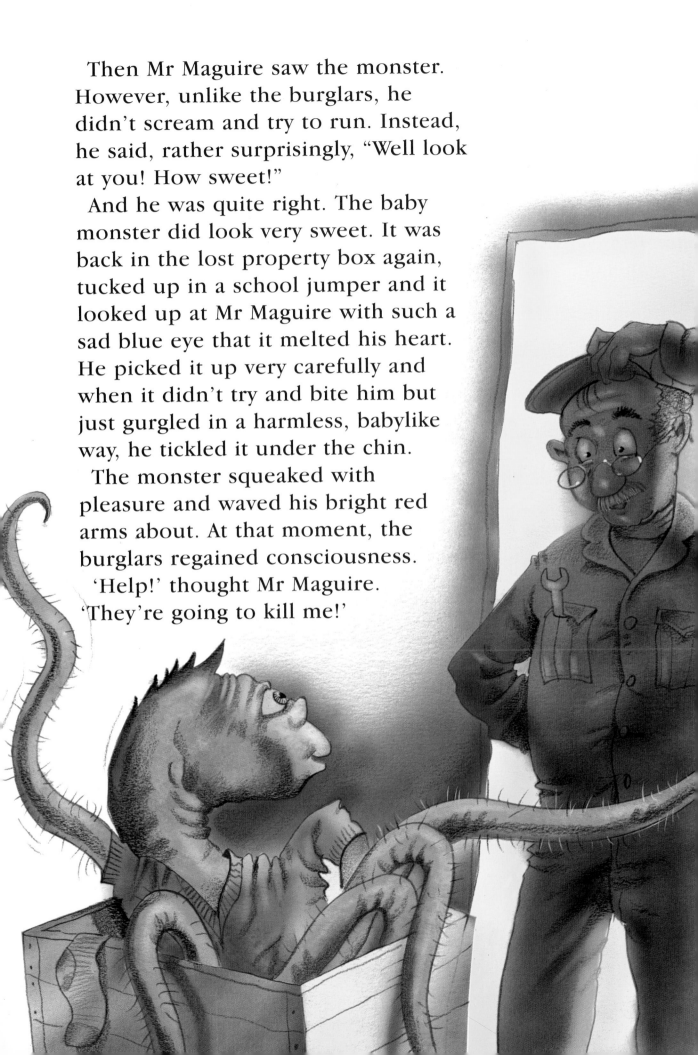

Then Mr Maguire saw the monster. However, unlike the burglars, he didn't scream and try to run. Instead, he said, rather surprisingly, "Well look at you! How sweet!"

And he was quite right. The baby monster did look very sweet. It was back in the lost property box again, tucked up in a school jumper and it looked up at Mr Maguire with such a sad blue eye that it melted his heart. He picked it up very carefully and when it didn't try and bite him but just gurgled in a harmless, babylike way, he tickled it under the chin.

The monster squeaked with pleasure and waved his bright red arms about. At that moment, the burglars regained consciousness.

'Help!' thought Mr Maguire. 'They're going to kill me!'

But he needn't have worried. The two large men took one look at the baby monster, screamed in terror and ran for their lives.

That's when Mr Maguire had an extremely good idea.

"You would make a wonderful security guard," he told the monster. "I'll make you a nice home here and you can stop St Stephen's from being burgled again."

And that's exactly what happened. Mr Maguire told Miss Brown, the head teacher, all about the burglars and she agreed it would be very useful to have a monster to guard the school. Then, Miss Brown called a special assembly and introduced the baby monster to everyone. Like Mr Maguire and Miss Brown – but not

like the burglars, of course – they saw what a friendly little creature it was and they all wanted him to stay. After much debate, they named him Mortimer.

At first they were anxious that Mortimer wouldn't be scary enough to frighten intruders away, but they soon changed their minds when he started to grow. After one month of school food, Mortimer was too big for the games cupboard and by the next month, he was too big to get through the front door of the school. Luckily, he stopped growing then!

Everyone agreed that St Stephen's monster was the best thing that had ever happened. No-one ever guessed how Mortimer came to be there, not even little Jimmy Roberts – and he found him!

Dinosaurs!

Dinosaurs! Dinosaurs! All round my house,
  You're lucky if all that you've got is a mouse!
  I first knew my luck one night in the Spring,
When just after midnight the doorbell went DING!

I put on the chain and opened a crack,
What I saw on the porch really took me aback.
A tyrannosaur and a triceratops,
Were standing outside with grins on their chops.

"We want to come in!" they bellowed together,
"We're chilly out here – it's terrible weather!"
"Don't be silly," I yelled, "Can't you both see?
If you all squeeze in here there'll be no space for me!"

"There's only two rooms and they're both really small,
I don't think you'd even fit into the hall!"
It ended like this – I went back to bed,
With the dinosaurs snoring away in my shed!

Two Heads Are Worse Than One

Clay and Rye were fed up. They were fed up with their bossy parents, always giving them jobs to do. It was 'bring those turnips in,' and 'have you fed the chickens?' from dawn till dusk. So, one evening, Clay and Rye decided to run away. As darkness crept in, they crept out, away from the village and across the fields.

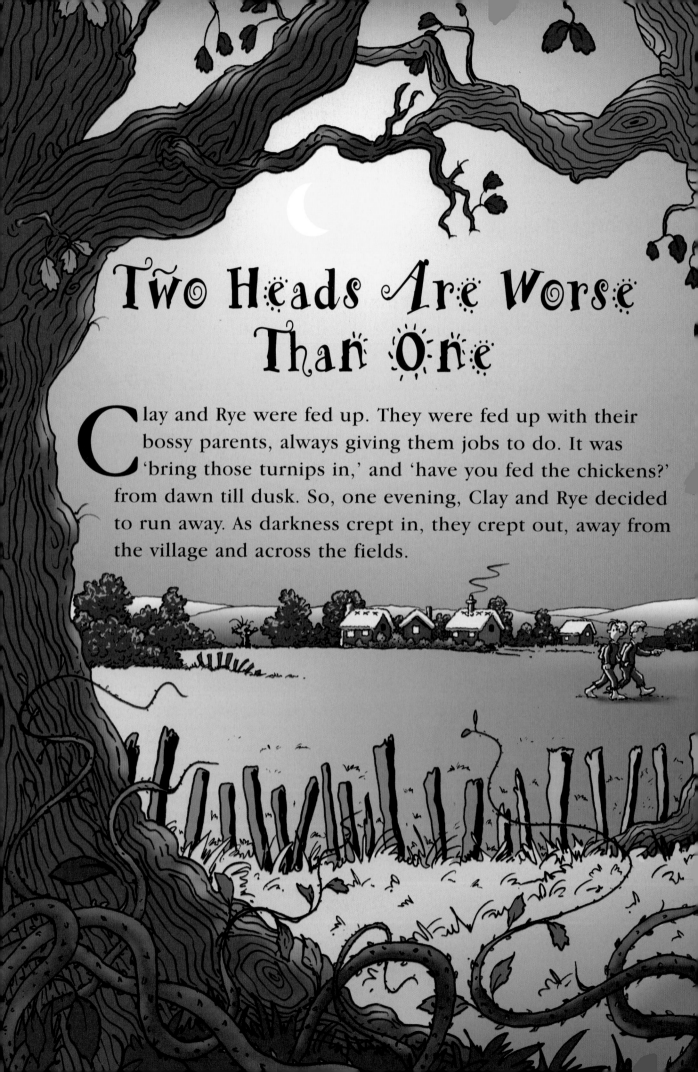

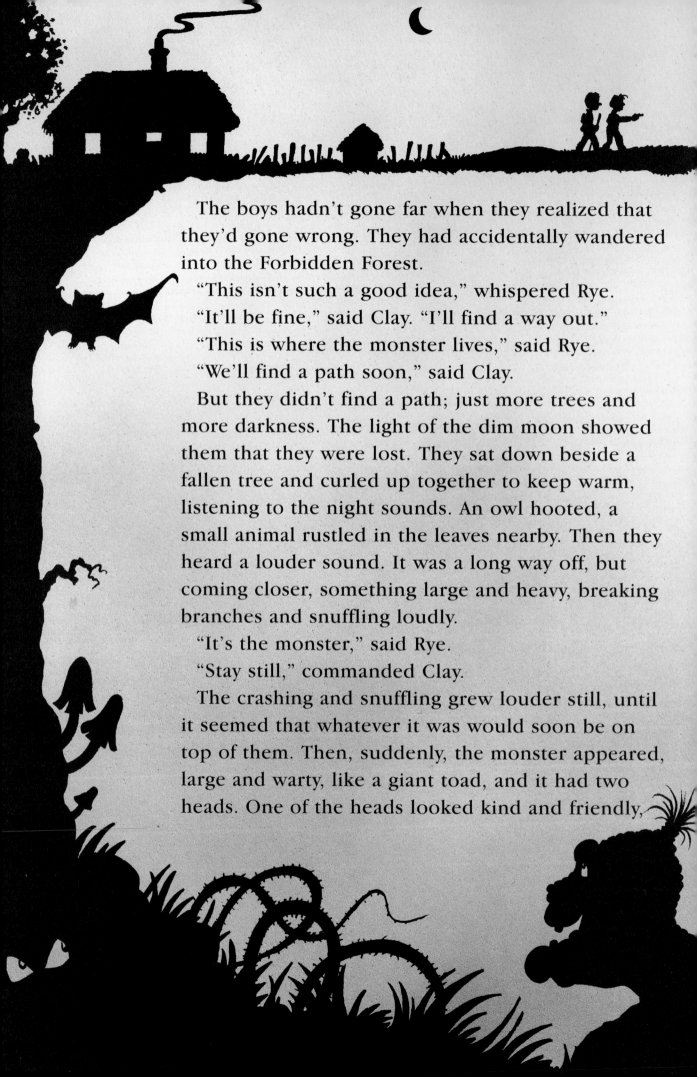

The boys hadn't gone far when they realized that they'd gone wrong. They had accidentally wandered into the Forbidden Forest.

"This isn't such a good idea," whispered Rye.

"It'll be fine," said Clay. "I'll find a way out."

"This is where the monster lives," said Rye.

"We'll find a path soon," said Clay.

But they didn't find a path; just more trees and more darkness. The light of the dim moon showed them that they were lost. They sat down beside a fallen tree and curled up together to keep warm, listening to the night sounds. An owl hooted, a small animal rustled in the leaves nearby. Then they heard a louder sound. It was a long way off, but coming closer, something large and heavy, breaking branches and snuffling loudly.

"It's the monster," said Rye.

"Stay still," commanded Clay.

The crashing and snuffling grew louder still, until it seemed that whatever it was would soon be on top of them. Then, suddenly, the monster appeared, large and warty, like a giant toad, and it had two heads. One of the heads looked kind and friendly,

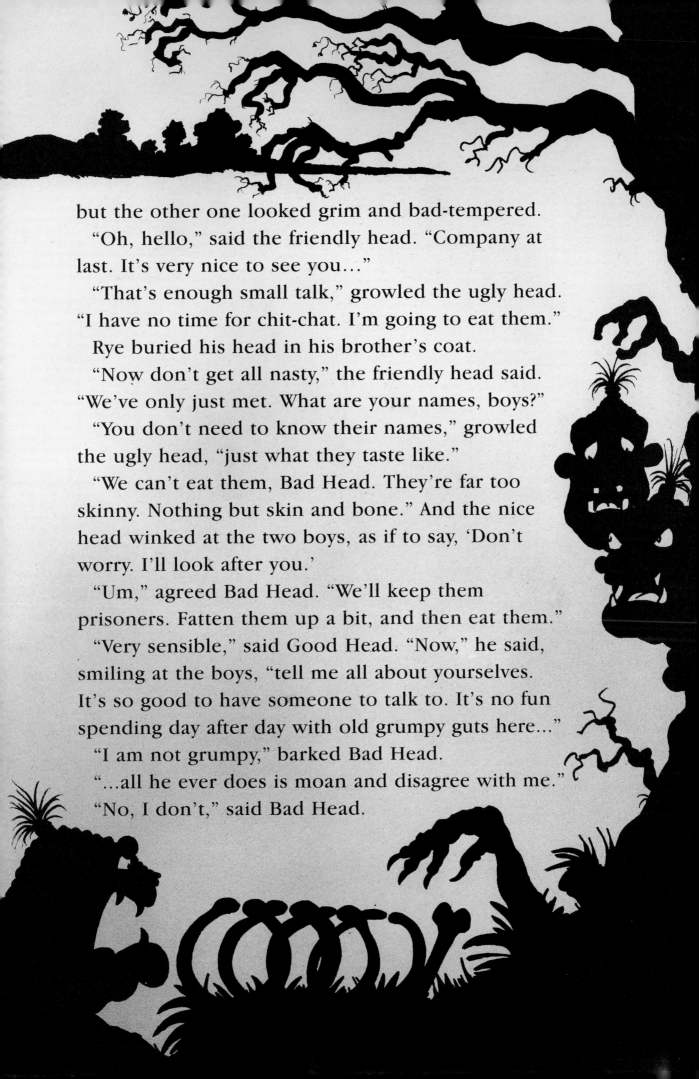

but the other one looked grim and bad-tempered.

"Oh, hello," said the friendly head. "Company at last. It's very nice to see you…"

"That's enough small talk," growled the ugly head. "I have no time for chit-chat. I'm going to eat them."

Rye buried his head in his brother's coat.

"Now don't get all nasty," the friendly head said. "We've only just met. What are your names, boys?"

"You don't need to know their names," growled the ugly head, "just what they taste like."

"We can't eat them, Bad Head. They're far too skinny. Nothing but skin and bone." And the nice head winked at the two boys, as if to say, 'Don't worry. I'll look after you.'

"Um," agreed Bad Head. "We'll keep them prisoners. Fatten them up a bit, and then eat them."

"Very sensible," said Good Head. "Now," he said, smiling at the boys, "tell me all about yourselves. It's so good to have someone to talk to. It's no fun spending day after day with old grumpy guts here…"

"I am not grumpy," barked Bad Head.

"…all he ever does is moan and disagree with me."

"No, I don't," said Bad Head.

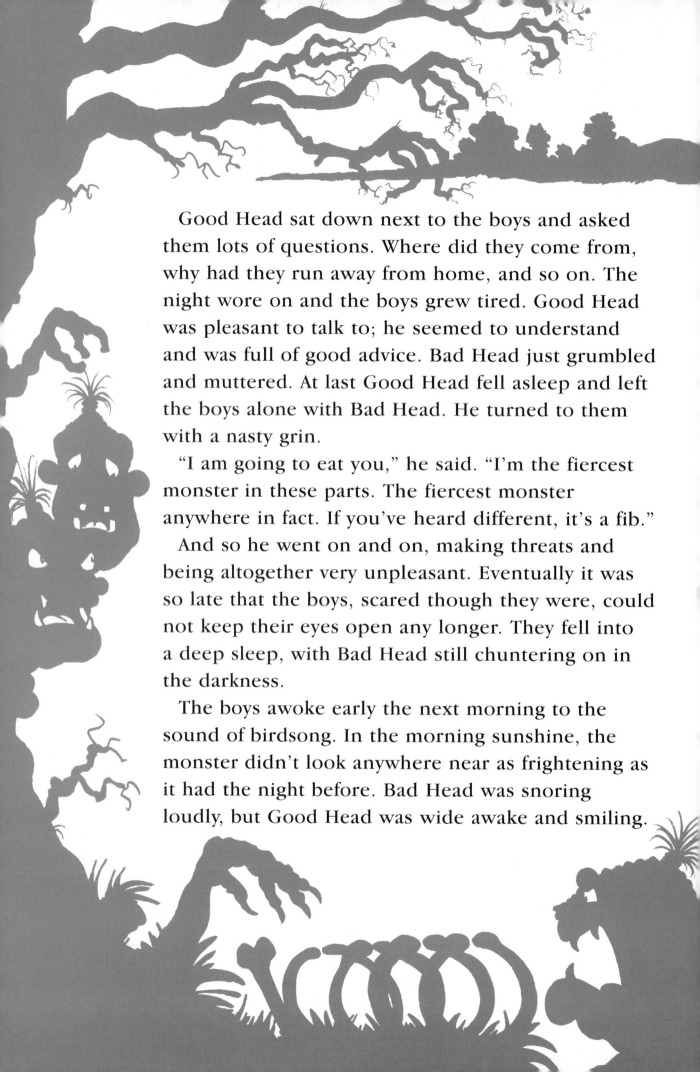

Good Head sat down next to the boys and asked
them lots of questions. Where did they come from,
why had they run away from home, and so on. The
night wore on and the boys grew tired. Good Head
was pleasant to talk to; he seemed to understand
and was full of good advice. Bad Head just grumbled
and muttered. At last Good Head fell asleep and left
the boys alone with Bad Head. He turned to them
with a nasty grin.

"I am going to eat you," he said. "I'm the fiercest
monster in these parts. The fiercest monster
anywhere in fact. If you've heard different, it's a fib."

And so he went on and on, making threats and
being altogether very unpleasant. Eventually it was
so late that the boys, scared though they were, could
not keep their eyes open any longer. They fell into
a deep sleep, with Bad Head still chuntering on in
the darkness.

The boys awoke early the next morning to the
sound of birdsong. In the morning sunshine, the
monster didn't look anywhere near as frightening as
it had the night before. Bad Head was snoring
loudly, but Good Head was wide awake and smiling.

"Did you sleep well?" he whispered. "Sorry it's so uncomfortable. I have been meaning to build a little cabin or something, with comfy beds, but it's so hard to get anything done with Old Misery here. I could lead you back to the village, but he'll be awake soon, so we'll do it tonight."

And Good Head told the boys how he was going to save them. After a day in the forest, foraging for food to fatten up the boys, the monster would be very tired. When they sat down in the evening, the boys should sing a soothing lullaby. That would lull Bad Head to sleep and while he slept, Good Head would lead them to safety.

"Won't it make you sleepy, too?" asked Rye.

"You could put something in your ears," suggested Clay. "Then you won't hear us and you'll stay awake."

They all agreed that it was a good idea, but just then, Bad Head woke up.

"Is it morning already?" he grumbled. "I feel terrible. I'm cold and hungry."

They all spent a busy day in the forest, looking for food. Good Head showed them which berries and roots were safe to eat.

When evening fell, they sat beside a warm fire and talked. Good Head said that having to feed a few chickens wasn't such a bad thing if you had a warm house to live in and a soft bed, and the boys had to agree that the life they'd run away from wasn't so bad after all.

"What nonsense," grumbled Bad Head, rather sleepily.

Good Head winked at the boys; it was their sign to begin singing, while Good Head carefully rolled up some leaves and stuffed them into his ears.

The boys started to sing a lullaby:

"Rock a bye baby,
On the tree top.
When the wind blows,
The cradle will rock."

Bad Head's eyes closed for a moment and then jerked open again. "Rubbish," he muttered.

"When the bough breaks,
The cradle will fall.
Down will come baby,
Cradle and all."

It worked. Bad Head was fast asleep. He was lolling forward and snoring once more.
"Quickly," whispered Good Head.
They rose to their feet and hurried as fast, but as quietly as they could, out of the forest.

When they reached the edge the boys turned to Good Head.

"Thank you," they whispered.

"My pleasure," said Good Head. "Now hurry."

Clay and Rye scampered across the open fields towards home. After a little while, they stopped because they could hear voices.

"What's going on?" asked Bad Head.

"The boys," said Good Head. "They got away."

"They got away!" shouted Bad Head. "You useless monster. Why didn't you stop them?"

"They were too fast," said Good Head. "Anyway, you weren't a lot of help, snoring away…"

"What can we eat now?" grumbled Bad Head.

The voices faded away into the forest and the boys ran gratefully home. They would have some explaining to do when they got back, but then they would put the chickens away for the night and snuggle up thankfully into their own soft, cosy beds.

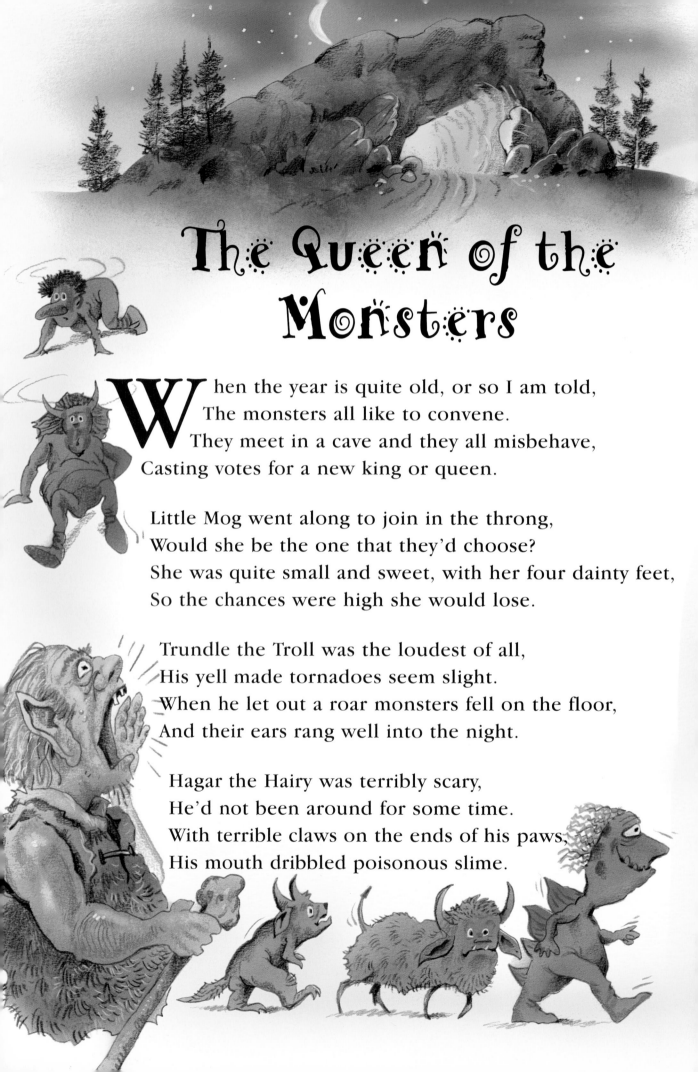

The Queen of the Monsters

When the year is quite old, or so I am told,
The monsters all like to convene.
They meet in a cave and they all misbehave,
Casting votes for a new king or queen.

Little Mog went along to join in the throng,
Would she be the one that they'd choose?
She was quite small and sweet, with her four dainty feet,
So the chances were high she would lose.

Trundle the Troll was the loudest of all,
His yell made tornadoes seem slight.
When he let out a roar monsters fell on the floor,
And their ears rang well into the night.

Hagar the Hairy was terribly scary,
He'd not been around for some time.
With terrible claws on the ends of his paws,
His mouth dribbled poisonous slime.

Whiffpong the Stinker, not much of a thinker,
Had a pong that made strong monsters flee.
His terrible breath could just stink you to death,
And his armpits could wither a tree.

Most monstrous of all was Slod the Slimeball,
Her warts were a perfect disgrace.
Her favourite ruse was to let out an ooze,
So you'd slip up all over the place.

The monsters agreed, as they sat down to feed,
That Slod was the one they'd all dread.
But who'd want a fiend for a monstrous queen?
So they all voted Mog in instead.

Alien Exchange

"James, hurry up!"

James stretched and opened one sleepy eye.

"Time for school," called his mum.

James groaned. He didn't like school. School was boring. He wanted to be an astronaut and they didn't teach you how to do that at school, at least not at St Maud's Junior School. James pulled the duvet up under his nose. He liked his bed. He liked his bedroom. Mum had painted the ceiling midnight blue and they had both stuck up hundreds of luminous stars which beamed down at him.

On the wall were paintings of the planets.
James knew all about space. In fact, his teacher
said his head was full of it. On the shelves were
books about the Galaxy, U.F.Os, rockets and
space travel, and he had a weird and wonderful
lava lamp on his desk, with his collection of
alien figures. There were gold ones, silver ones,
even inflatable ones. Some played tunes, some
had flashing eyes, some glowed in the dark –
all of them were very special.

"James you are going to miss the school bus
if you don't get a move on." His mum's voice
disturbed his thoughts and reluctantly James
slid out of bed and into his school uniform.
He was just about to leave the room when
something made him turn. Out of the corner
of his eye he felt sure he saw one of the figures
move. He walked over to the desk to examine
them more closely. Yes, the smallest green alien
at the front had definitely turned and was facing

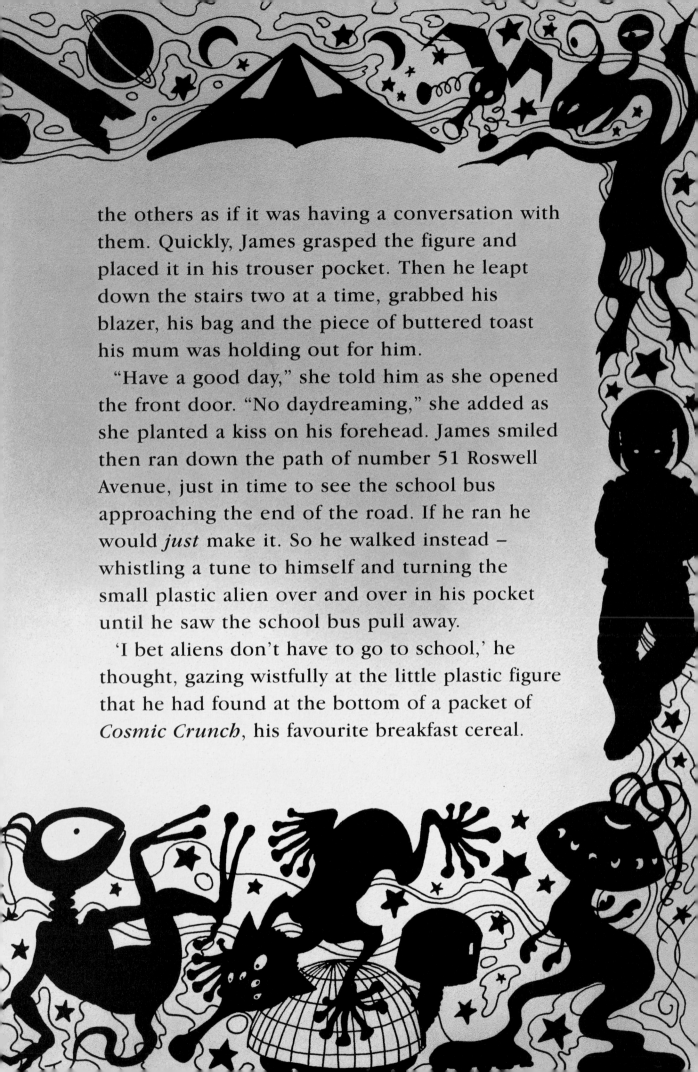

the others as if it was having a conversation with them. Quickly, James grasped the figure and placed it in his trouser pocket. Then he leapt down the stairs two at a time, grabbed his blazer, his bag and the piece of buttered toast his mum was holding out for him.

"Have a good day," she told him as she opened the front door. "No daydreaming," she added as she planted a kiss on his forehead. James smiled then ran down the path of number 51 Roswell Avenue, just in time to see the school bus approaching the end of the road. If he ran he would *just* make it. So he walked instead – whistling a tune to himself and turning the small plastic alien over and over in his pocket until he saw the school bus pull away.

'I bet aliens don't have to go to school,' he thought, gazing wistfully at the little plastic figure that he had found at the bottom of a packet of *Cosmic Crunch*, his favourite breakfast cereal.

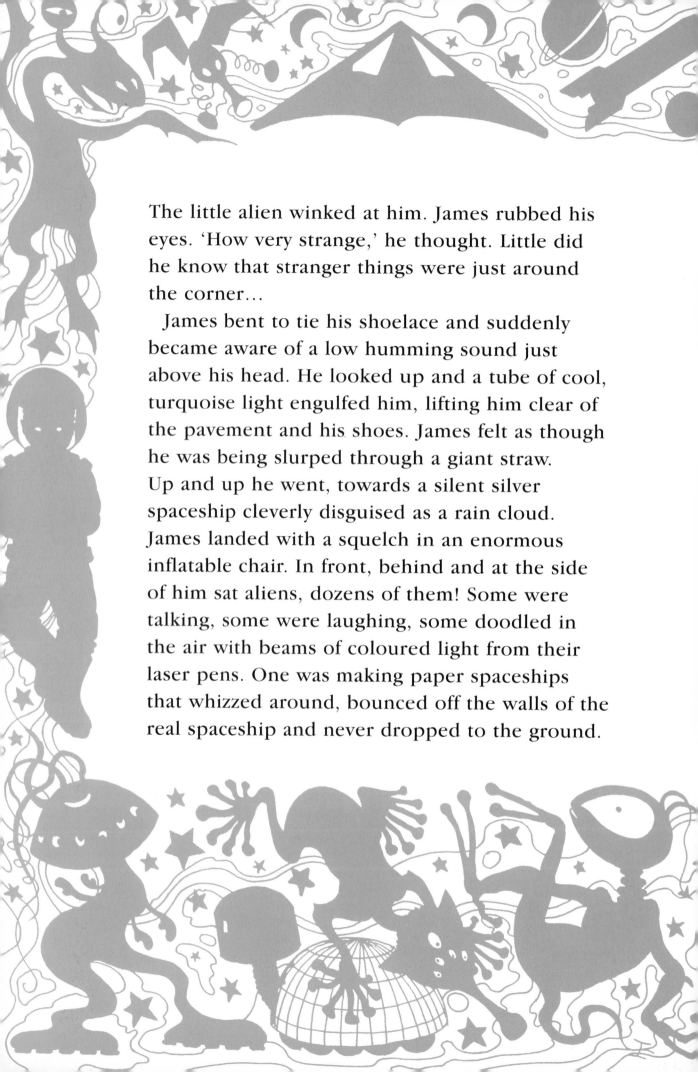

The little alien winked at him. James rubbed his eyes. 'How very strange,' he thought. Little did he know that stranger things were just around the corner…

James bent to tie his shoelace and suddenly became aware of a low humming sound just above his head. He looked up and a tube of cool, turquoise light engulfed him, lifting him clear of the pavement and his shoes. James felt as though he was being slurped through a giant straw. Up and up he went, towards a silent silver spaceship cleverly disguised as a rain cloud. James landed with a squelch in an enormous inflatable chair. In front, behind and at the side of him sat aliens, dozens of them! Some were talking, some were laughing, some doodled in the air with beams of coloured light from their laser pens. One was making paper spaceships that whizzed around, bounced off the walls of the real spaceship and never dropped to the ground.

James blinked in disbelief. He was on a spaceship full of aliens, real aliens. Suddenly a door swooshed open and a tall, serious-looking alien in a shimmering mortar board and gown glided in. "Good morning class," he began, "I'd like you all to welcome earthling James who will be joining us on the school ship today."

The alien extended a three-fingered hand and pointed at James. He could feel row upon row of big, bright almond eyes staring curiously at him and he had the strangest feeling that he was the alien.

"It's cool to meet a real earthling," said a small alien sitting opposite James. "I collect all the figures, look." He fished in the little silver pouch around his waist and pulled out a plastic figure of a boy that looked remarkably like James, except that it was only two inches tall. James began to laugh and pulled out his own alien figure.

"We should swop them as souvenirs," suggested the alien – so they did.

Afternoon school passed all too quickly. James was asked to talk to the whole class about life on Earth. He told the aliens about his wonderful space bedroom, his mum and dad, his pet dog Orion. The aliens listened with interest. James told them about school, all his friends and how when he grew up he wanted to be an astronaut.

Professor Zero patted him on the back.

"Thank you, thank you," he smiled, "I'm sure if you work hard at your Earth lessons then one day you will be an astronaut and perhaps you will visit us again."

James nodded eagerly – then felt the tiniest twinge of guilt as he remembered that he should have been at school today. He glanced out of the spaceship window. There he could see the familiar green and blue patches of Earth as they hurtled towards it.

The alien children gathered round to say goodbye to their new friend as a trap door opened in the floor of the spaceship ready to beam him back down to Earth.

"Three cheers for James," called Professor Zero and the aliens raised their arms.

"Hip hip."

"Hooray."

"Hip hip."

"Hooray."

"Hip hip."

"Hooray."

"HOORAY, hooray … HHHHurry up."

James opened his eyes with a start.

"Hurry up James, you'll be late for school."

Reality made James' head spin. He was in bed, in his pyjamas. The aliens, Professor Zero, the school ship, had all been part of a marvellous dream. Sadly James clambered out of bed, it all seemed so real.

James began to unbutton his pyjamas thinking sadly that he'd never get to see the aliens again because they didn't really exist. Then he spotted something out of the corner of his eye. There on the desk, right in the middle of his alien collection, stood the small plastic figure of a boy, just like him. James smiled a broad smile.

"You'll miss the bus if you don't hurry James," called his mum.

"No I won't," replied James, pulling on his school shirt. He stared at the figure on his desk and he was sure, absolutely certain, that it winked at him.

Rainbow Rescue

Rosa's grandpa was an inventor. He had wiry grey hair, a large handlebar moustache and when he was busy inventing – which was most of the time – he always wore a white coat. Grandpa had most of his ideas and built most of his inventions in a tumble-down shed down at the bottom of the garden. Rosa thought it was the most exciting place in the world.

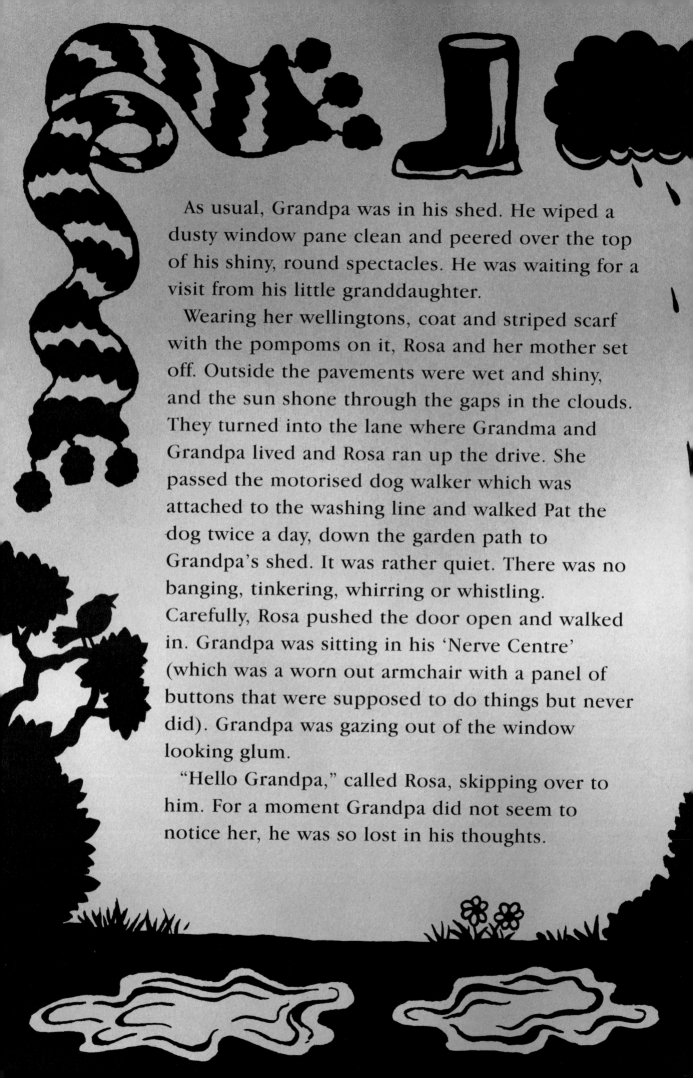

As usual, Grandpa was in his shed. He wiped a
dusty window pane clean and peered over the top
of his shiny, round spectacles. He was waiting for a
visit from his little granddaughter.

Wearing her wellingtons, coat and striped scarf
with the pompoms on it, Rosa and her mother set
off. Outside the pavements were wet and shiny,
and the sun shone through the gaps in the clouds.
They turned into the lane where Grandma and
Grandpa lived and Rosa ran up the drive. She
passed the motorised dog walker which was
attached to the washing line and walked Pat the
dog twice a day, down the garden path to
Grandpa's shed. It was rather quiet. There was no
banging, tinkering, whirring or whistling.
Carefully, Rosa pushed the door open and walked
in. Grandpa was sitting in his 'Nerve Centre'
(which was a worn out armchair with a panel of
buttons that were supposed to do things but never
did). Grandpa was gazing out of the window
looking glum.

"Hello Grandpa," called Rosa, skipping over to
him. For a moment Grandpa did not seem to
notice her, he was so lost in his thoughts.

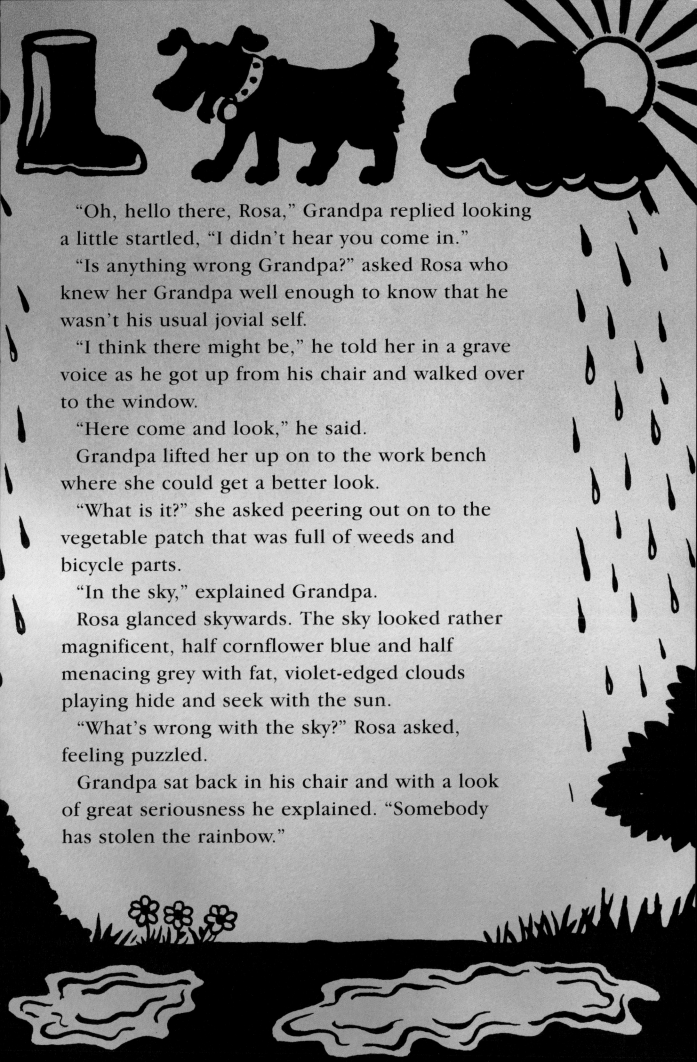

"Oh, hello there, Rosa," Grandpa replied looking a little startled, "I didn't hear you come in."

"Is anything wrong Grandpa?" asked Rosa who knew her Grandpa well enough to know that he wasn't his usual jovial self.

"I think there might be," he told her in a grave voice as he got up from his chair and walked over to the window.

"Here come and look," he said.

Grandpa lifted her up on to the work bench where she could get a better look.

"What is it?" she asked peering out on to the vegetable patch that was full of weeds and bicycle parts.

"In the sky," explained Grandpa.

Rosa glanced skywards. The sky looked rather magnificent, half cornflower blue and half menacing grey with fat, violet-edged clouds playing hide and seek with the sun.

"What's wrong with the sky?" Rosa asked, feeling puzzled.

Grandpa sat back in his chair and with a look of great seriousness he explained. "Somebody has stolen the rainbow."

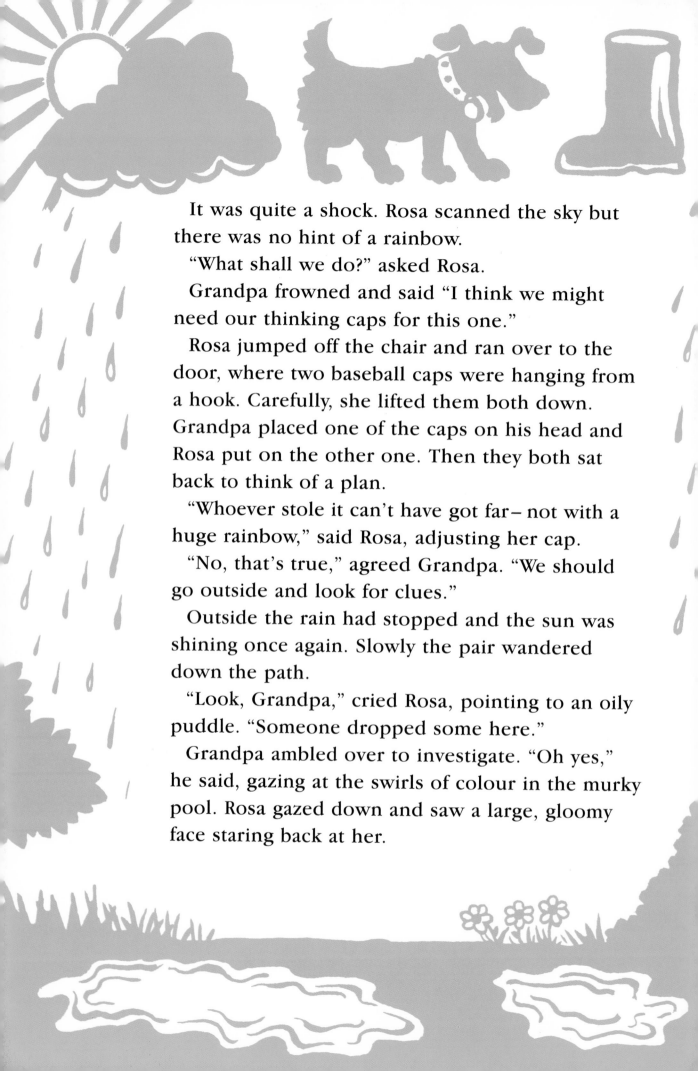

It was quite a shock. Rosa scanned the sky but there was no hint of a rainbow.

"What shall we do?" asked Rosa.

Grandpa frowned and said "I think we might need our thinking caps for this one."

Rosa jumped off the chair and ran over to the door, where two baseball caps were hanging from a hook. Carefully, she lifted them both down. Grandpa placed one of the caps on his head and Rosa put on the other one. Then they both sat back to think of a plan.

"Whoever stole it can't have got far– not with a huge rainbow," said Rosa, adjusting her cap.

"No, that's true," agreed Grandpa. "We should go outside and look for clues."

Outside the rain had stopped and the sun was shining once again. Slowly the pair wandered down the path.

"Look, Grandpa," cried Rosa, pointing to an oily puddle. "Someone dropped some here."

Grandpa ambled over to investigate. "Oh yes," he said, gazing at the swirls of colour in the murky pool. Rosa gazed down and saw a large, gloomy face staring back at her.

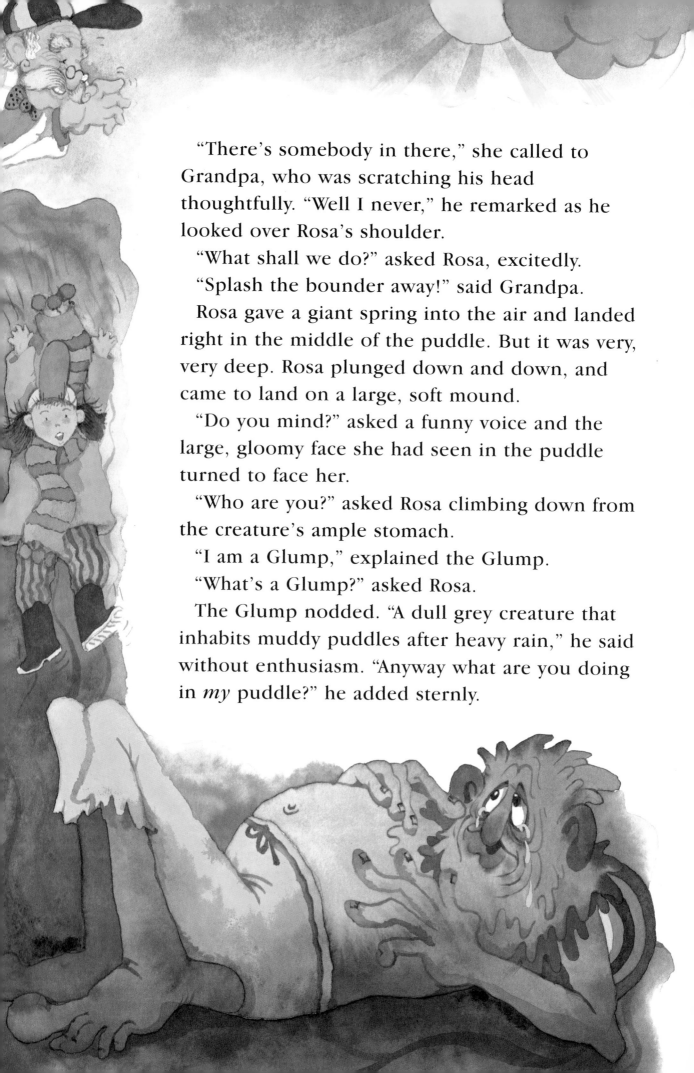

"There's somebody in there," she called to Grandpa, who was scratching his head thoughtfully. "Well I never," he remarked as he looked over Rosa's shoulder.

"What shall we do?" asked Rosa, excitedly.

"Splash the bounder away!" said Grandpa.

Rosa gave a giant spring into the air and landed right in the middle of the puddle. But it was very, very deep. Rosa plunged down and down, and came to land on a large, soft mound.

"Do you mind?" asked a funny voice and the large, gloomy face she had seen in the puddle turned to face her.

"Who are you?" asked Rosa climbing down from the creature's ample stomach.

"I am a Glump," explained the Glump.

"What's a Glump?" asked Rosa.

The Glump nodded. "A dull grey creature that inhabits muddy puddles after heavy rain," he said without enthusiasm. "Anyway what are you doing in *my* puddle?" he added sternly.

"I'm looking for the rainbow," Rosa explained.

"A rainbow," he said, shuffling nervously from one large foot to the other, and Rosa was certain she saw a glimpse of red peeping out over the Glump's broad shoulder.

"What are you hiding?" she asked suspiciously.

"Hiding?" he said, turning from side to side as Rosa attempted to look behind him.

But Rosa was too quick for the dull, sluggish Glump and suddenly she was standing right behind him. "Caught red-handed!" she exclaimed triumphantly, "and orange and yellow and green and blue and indigo and violet."

The Glump hung his head in shame as Rosa leaned against the glorious rainbow. Then, much to her surprise, he began to cry.

"I just wanted some colour in my life," wailed the Glump, "I didn't think anyone would miss it," he explained, blowing his nose very loudly.

"Not miss a rainbow!" scolded Rosa wagging a finger at him, which made him cry even more.

"Oh, do stop," insisted Rosa. "Look I'll tell you what, I'll swap you this for the rainbow."

The Glump stopped crying, picked up the multicoloured scarf and placed it around his own neck. "Like a sort of present," he said.

"Yes," Rosa told him, "a present in exchange for the rainbow."

The Glump sniffed loudly then, stroking the scarf, he smiled a broad smile.

"Thank you *very* much," he said.

"You're welcome," Rosa told him. "You should smile more often you don't look nearly so dreary when you do."

"Really?" he asked, practising a smile.

"The rainbow– please?" Rosa asked him.

"Oh, yes, of course," he replied and then with an almighty throw, he hurled the rainbow upwards out of the puddle. Rosa's eyes followed it as it spun over and over, crossing the sky. The sun was shining more brightly than ever now and the edges of the Glump's puddle were starting to shrink. As they did, the monster grew smaller and his voice grew weaker as he thanked her again and again until he vanished completely.

Rosa looked around. Grandpa was standing scratching his head. "Well I never," he was saying, "fancy losing your scarf in a puddle!"

Then as the rain started to fall again they both looked up at the sky just in time to see the biggest, brightest rainbow ever.

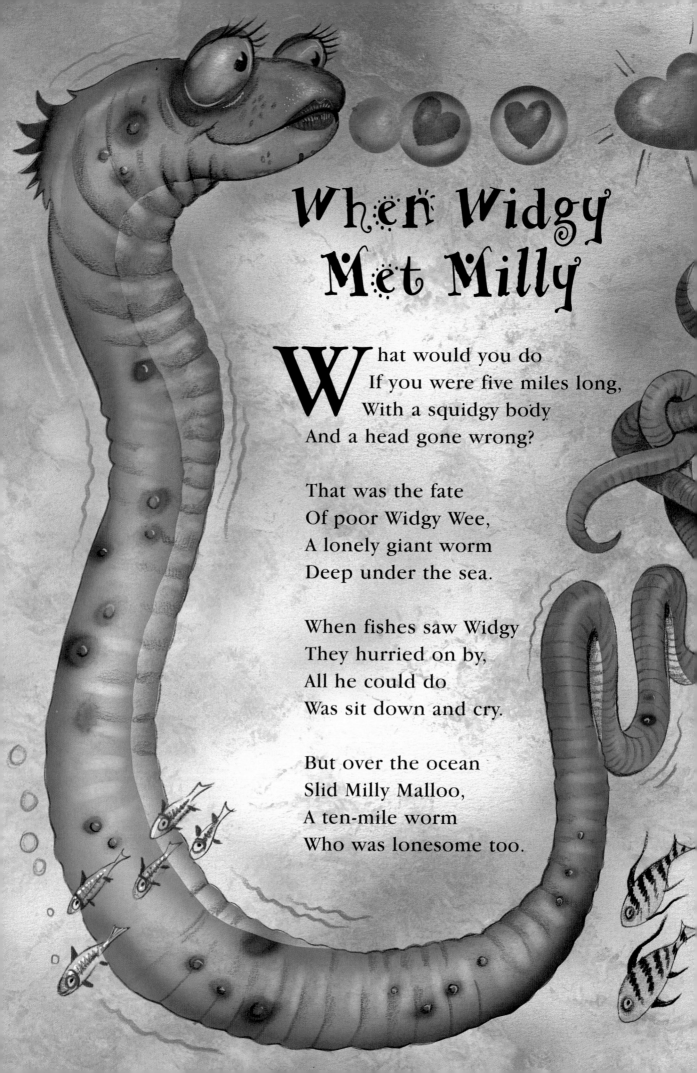

When Widgy Met Milly

What would you do
If you were five miles long,
With a squidgy body
And a head gone wrong?

That was the fate
Of poor Widgy Wee,
A lonely giant worm
Deep under the sea.

When fishes saw Widgy
They hurried on by,
All he could do
Was sit down and cry.

But over the ocean
Slid Milly Malloo,
A ten-mile worm
Who was lonesome too.

The sea witch had told her
About Widgy Wee,
Said Milly Malloo
"That's the worm for me!"

When Widgy met Milly
It was love at first sight,
Though all of the fish
Swam away in fright.

"Be mine!" cried Widgy
"We're all that we've got!"
"I will!" beamed Milly.
And they both tied the knot.

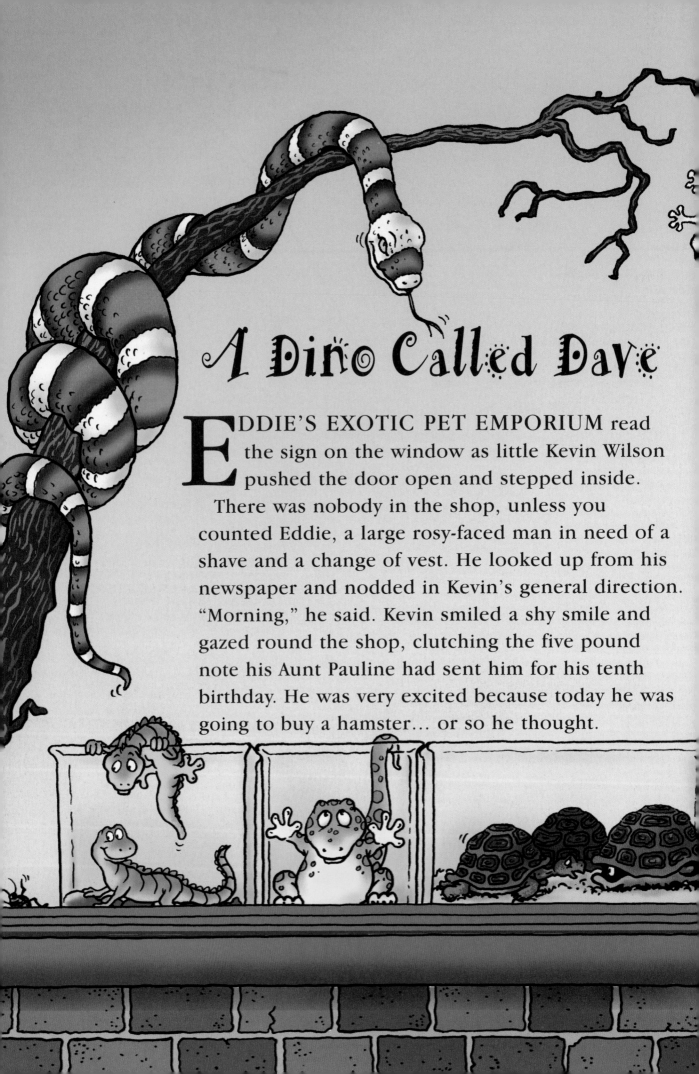

A Dino Called Dave

EDDIE'S EXOTIC PET EMPORIUM read
the sign on the window as little Kevin Wilson
pushed the door open and stepped inside.
There was nobody in the shop, unless you
counted Eddie, a large rosy-faced man in need of a
shave and a change of vest. He looked up from his
newspaper and nodded in Kevin's general direction.
"Morning," he said. Kevin smiled a shy smile and
gazed round the shop, clutching the five pound
note his Aunt Pauline had sent him for his tenth
birthday. He was very excited because today he was
going to buy a hamster... or so he thought.

"WOW!" There were wall-to-wall tanks containing weird and wonderful creatures; lizards, snakes, spiders and amazing shimmering tropical fish. On the counter sat a large, impressive parrot, who was reciting the alphabet backwards whilst eating a grape. But there was very little in the way of hamsters, in fact there were *no* hamsters.

Eddie folded his newspaper in half and scratched his armpit. A bewildered dung beetle fell out and scurried across the counter.

"Were you looking for something special?" he asked the small, pasty-faced boy.

"Do you have any hamsters?" Kevin asked meekly.

Eddie shook his head and a couple of sleepy locusts fell out of his hair onto the floor.

"There are no hamsters in here," he said, "unless they're lost." Then, slowly, he turned to the hand painted sign behind his head and with a fat finger pointed to the words 'EXOTIC' and 'PET'.

Kevin had been given strict instructions to buy a

hamster and nothing else, but now, surrounded by so many splendid and exciting creatures, he found himself wondering what it might be like to be the owner of a tarantula, or a chameleon or an Indian python or in fact all three.

Since he and his mum had moved to the area, he had been rather lonely. He had not made many friends at his new school yet and he didn't think he ever would. Nobody seemed to notice a thin, bespectacled boy, small for his age and with a mop of curly hair, except the school bully, Grizzly Greaves, who teased him mercilessly. Kevin imagined what life would be like if he had an Indian python. Would you pick on a boy whose best friend was a python?

"You like snakes do you?" asked Eddie. He looked enormous as he appeared from behind the counter. Kevin looked up and nodded nervously. Eddie smiled a yellow smile. "He will cost a few weeks pocket money," Eddie told him, pointing to the tatty price label in the top corner of the tank.

If the creatures in Eddie's Exotic Pet Emporium were fantastic, which they were, their price tags were even more so. It appeared all poor Kevin could afford was an angelfish or a large bag of Deluxe Parrot Mix, Tropical Blend. He sighed and made his way to the door.

Eddie smiled to himself and called after the small boy. "Of course, if you're looking for something really special…"

Kevin turned to see Eddie reaching below the counter and taking out a small plastic tank in which there sat, perfectly still, a tiny, lizard-like creature.

"What is it?" whispered Kevin, peering over the top of his spectacles.

"That, my lad," said Eddie grandly "is a baby dinosaur."

Kevin stared hard at the thin neck and the dark, glossy body; he supposed it did look like a dinosaur, a miniature one of course.

Eddie gave the side of the tank a little tap and the creature turned and looked Kevin straight in the eye.

"It needs special care and attention," said Eddie, "but you look like a sensible lad."

"I am," nodded Kevin proudly. Usually sensible meant boring but Eddie used the word as if to be sensible was something special.

"How much is he?" asked Kevin crumpling the five pound note, and fearing the worst.

"Free to a good home," said Eddie, "I'll just jot down a few instructions then he's all yours."

Kevin could not believe it, his very own dinosaur! He said thank you, grasped the little container tightly under his arm and stuffed the care instructions into his pocket. Then, just as he reached the door, a thought wandered into his head.

"What is he called?" he asked, expecting Eddie to give him some long and complicated dinosaur name.

"He's called Dave," said Eddie, casually flipping his paper open and perching himself on a high stool.

"Never mind," said Kevin's mum as she met him outside the shop, "perhaps they'll have some hamsters next week." Kevin nodded and held on tightly to the little tank tucked inside his sweatshirt where his mother couldn't see it.

Dave had to live under Kevin's bed with the forgotten toys, odd socks and mouldy banana skins, but he didn't mind. His new owner was very kind, fed him twice a day, kept him clean and, late at night when the house was quiet, he would talk to him about his day at school.

School had been pretty uneventful that week. Kevin's teacher had forgotten his name three times, but Grizzly Greaves had only threatened him once so things seemed to be getting better. It was Friday afternoon and Kevin was sauntering along the corridor on his way to double maths when a poster on the notice board caught his eye.

'SHOW AND TELL CONTEST' Kevin read. The poster said the contest was to be held in the lecture theatre the following Thursday afternoon and there would be a prize for the most original talk.

Kevin would never normally have dared to enter such a competition, but he suddenly found himself filling in an entry form and where it said 'subject' he wrote in large capitals,

'MY PET DINOSAUR'

Thursday soon arrived and Kevin watched anxiously as the whole school filed into the lecture theatre. He was very nervous as he waited, but the moment he stood in front of the school with Dave sitting quietly in his tank on the table, he forgot all his fears.

Everyone listened, enthralled, as he talked about dinosaurs in general and then introduced Dave, who entertained everyone by doing a few of the tricks that Kevin had taught him. It was over all too soon and the whole school, including the teachers, were on their feet clapping and cheering. Kevin had never known such attention and he stood there grinning from ear to ear as his classmates came up to pat him on the back and get a closer look at Dave. Finally the Headmaster announced that Kevin was the overall winner and congratulated him on an imaginative and highly entertaining talk. First prize was a book voucher, it was the first time he had ever won a prize in his life!

Of course Kevin's mum was delighted to hear that Kevin had won, but rather disappointed that he had not told her about his unusual pet.

"Yes, he is sweet, Kevin," she said, "but he isn't a hamster." At first she said Dave must go back to the shop but when Kevin explained that he had been given Dave, his mum agreed that it would not be polite to return a gift. So the little creature was allowed to stay, provided Kevin did his homework every night and got to school on time every morning. Kevin found it easy to keep these promises. Since the Show and Tell Contest he was beginning to enjoy school, he'd made some new friends, the Headmaster no longer called him 'you boy', and even Grizzly Greaves had stopped taunting him.

On Saturday Kevin and his mum went to the book shop to spend the voucher. Naturally Kevin was looking for books on dinosaurs,

then he spotted a book with a picture of Dave on the front – well a creature very like him. Kevin opened the cover and read that the little shiny fellow was in fact a common newt. Well, fancy that! The old Kevin would have been very upset to learn that his unusual pet was nothing more than a common pond newt, he might have even cried, but not this Kevin. Dinosaur or not, Dave had brought him good luck and good friends and he was the best pet a boy could have.

Monster Munch

I may be big and hairy
And I may look mean and tough,
But I'm a nice, kind monster,
And I've simply had enough!

It's really most distressing
When you scream and run away—
I have no plans to eat you,
All I want to do is play!

Oh, can't you see I'm lonely?
Can't you tell I'm feeling blue?
I've got no friends to talk to,
But I like the look of you!

It really gets me down
To see you shake with fright,
For though I growl and slaver,
My bark's worse than my bite!

Don't let my dribble scare you,
Don't be put off by my eyes,
Take time to get to know me –
You'll be in for a surprise!

I'm just about to make some lunch,
And I'd love it if you'd come.
You will? Oh, great, that's perfect!
Ha, ha – I tricked you! – yum!

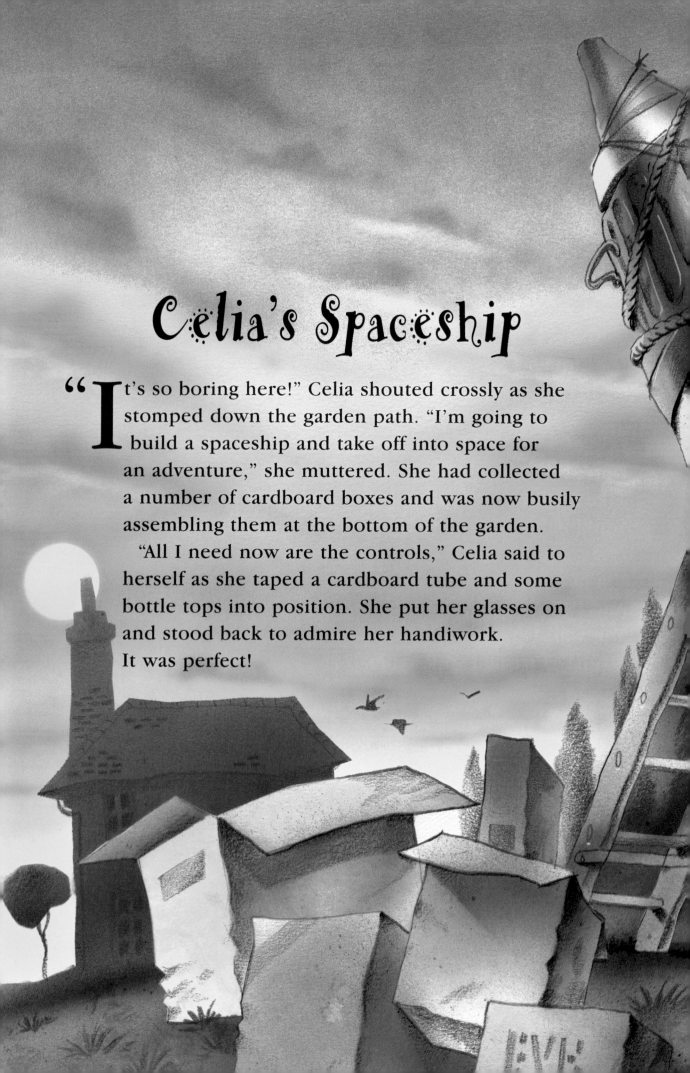

Celia's Spaceship

"It's so boring here!" Celia shouted crossly as she stomped down the garden path. "I'm going to build a spaceship and take off into space for an adventure," she muttered. She had collected a number of cardboard boxes and was now busily assembling them at the bottom of the garden.

"All I need now are the controls," Celia said to herself as she taped a cardboard tube and some bottle tops into position. She put her glasses on and stood back to admire her handiwork. It was perfect!

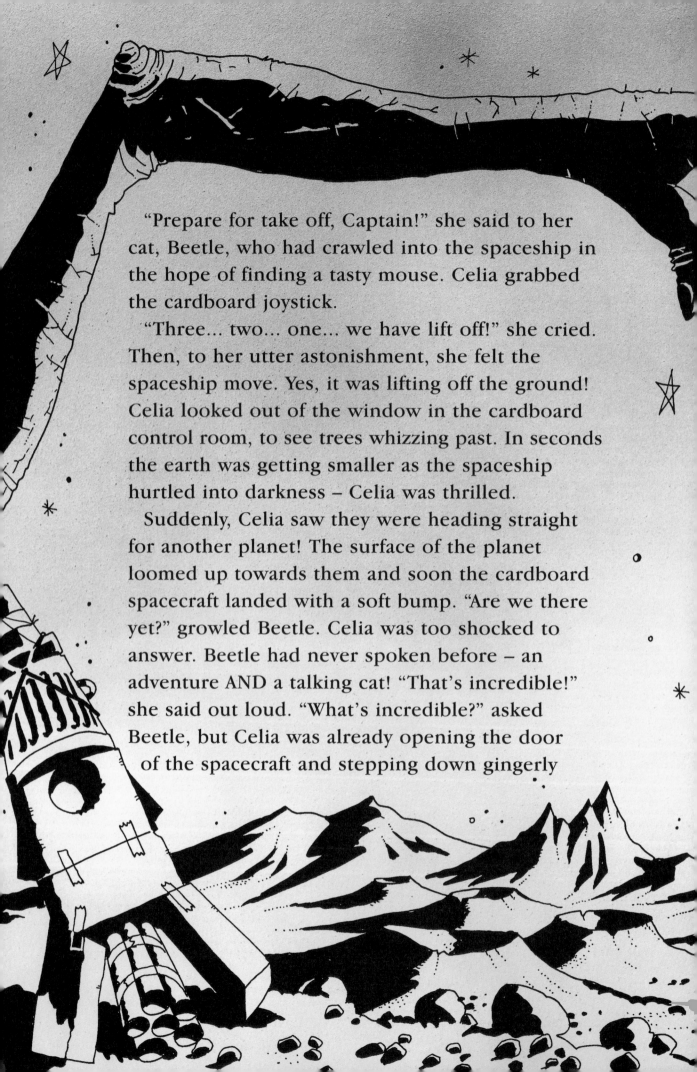

"Prepare for take off, Captain!" she said to her cat, Beetle, who had crawled into the spaceship in the hope of finding a tasty mouse. Celia grabbed the cardboard joystick.

"Three... two... one... we have lift off!" she cried. Then, to her utter astonishment, she felt the spaceship move. Yes, it was lifting off the ground! Celia looked out of the window in the cardboard control room, to see trees whizzing past. In seconds the earth was getting smaller as the spaceship hurtled into darkness – Celia was thrilled.

Suddenly, Celia saw they were heading straight for another planet! The surface of the planet loomed up towards them and soon the cardboard spacecraft landed with a soft bump. "Are we there yet?" growled Beetle. Celia was too shocked to answer. Beetle had never spoken before – an adventure AND a talking cat! "That's incredible!" she said out loud. "What's incredible?" asked Beetle, but Celia was already opening the door of the spacecraft and stepping down gingerly

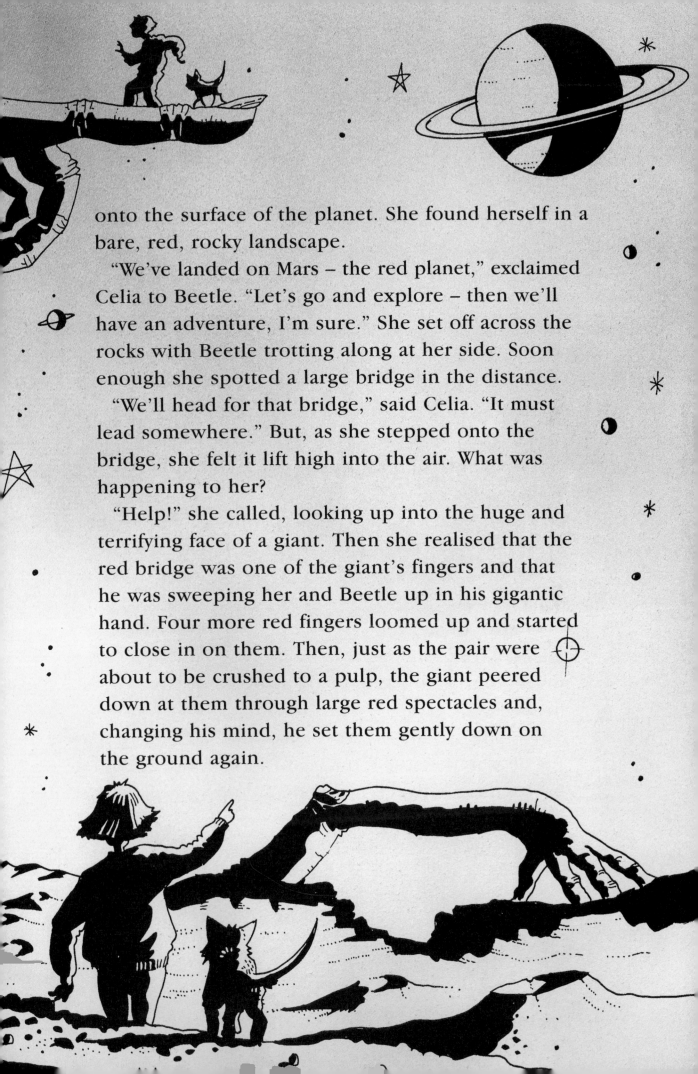

onto the surface of the planet. She found herself in a bare, red, rocky landscape.

"We've landed on Mars – the red planet," exclaimed Celia to Beetle. "Let's go and explore – then we'll have an adventure, I'm sure." She set off across the rocks with Beetle trotting along at her side. Soon enough she spotted a large bridge in the distance.

"We'll head for that bridge," said Celia. "It must lead somewhere." But, as she stepped onto the bridge, she felt it lift high into the air. What was happening to her?

"Help!" she called, looking up into the huge and terrifying face of a giant. Then she realised that the red bridge was one of the giant's fingers and that he was sweeping her and Beetle up in his gigantic hand. Four more red fingers loomed up and started to close in on them. Then, just as the pair were about to be crushed to a pulp, the giant peered down at them through large red spectacles and, changing his mind, he set them gently down on the ground again.

"Oh, dear!" he exclaimed, in a deep but rather shaky voice. "I'm so terribly sorry. I thought you were a couple of mice! The name's Red Giant, by the way. Pleased to meet you."

Celia looked up and noticed that the giant was very elderly indeed. Then she remembered something she'd read in a book about space. Red Giants – they were old stars, weren't they?

"I'm Beetle," the cat was saying. "And this is my friend Celia."

"I shall have to take you to my leader," Red Giant said. "He will decide what to do with you. If you're lucky, he'll let you go. If not…" Red Giant's voice trailed away.

"If not…what?" asked Celia. Red Giant slowly wiped a tear from his eye. "Well… I… I…" he began. Just then a small dark shape shot past between the giant's legs.

"Vermin!" shouted Red Giant. Quick as a flash, Beetle was after the mouse and was soon trotting back with it between his teeth.

"I say!" cried the giant, bending down to examine Beetle more closely. "Now you could be very useful. We've got a dreadful problem with mice round here. In the old days, I chased them myself. But now my eyesight's not what it was and they're just running out of control." Red Giant scratched his chin. "We'll tell the boss about your mousing skills and maybe everything'll be fine. Come along now!"

Before they could run away, Red Giant had swept the pair up in his hand again and was setting off across the planet. At last they reached the door of a red castle. The giant had to stoop quite low to avoid hitting the top of his head as he carried them inside.

Celia was set down in front of a strange-looking creature. It was very small and as

white as the giant was red. It had long flowing white hair and a straggly white beard.

"This is the chief." said Red Giant. "His name is White Dwarf. He's very old indeed. Ahem… even older than me, actually. And he is almost blind since he lost his glasses."

White Dwarf peered at Celia and Beetle. "What have we here?" he said, in a very menacing tone.

"Now White Dwarf, don't get cross," said Red Giant. "I know how you hate intruders…"

"Intruders, eh?" screamed White Dwarf, very angrily. "Throw them into the cells!"

Suddenly, Celia and Beetle found themselves surrounded by armed guards. They were marched down a dark tunnel to a dank cell, and chained inside. White Dwarf glared at them through the bars.

"That will teach you," he spat. "You can stay here till you rot!"

Just then, Red Giant spoke. "I think Beetle here could be really useful to have around, White Dwarf. He's very good at catching mice."

"A beetle!" exclaimed White Dwarf. "A beetle that can catch mice! Well, I..."

"No, no!" interrupted Red Giant. "He's a cat!"

"Very well," said White Dwarf, "I'll release him, but he'd better make a good job of it. The other creature will stay chained up."

So Beetle was dispatched to catch mice, while Celia sat in the cell. How could she ever escape? Then she had an idea.

"White Dwarf!" she called. "If you will release me, I will find you some glasses."

White Dwarf spun around. "What are you – a wizard? Is this a trick?"

"No!" cried Celia. "Trust me." She reached into her pocket and carefully pulled out her own pair

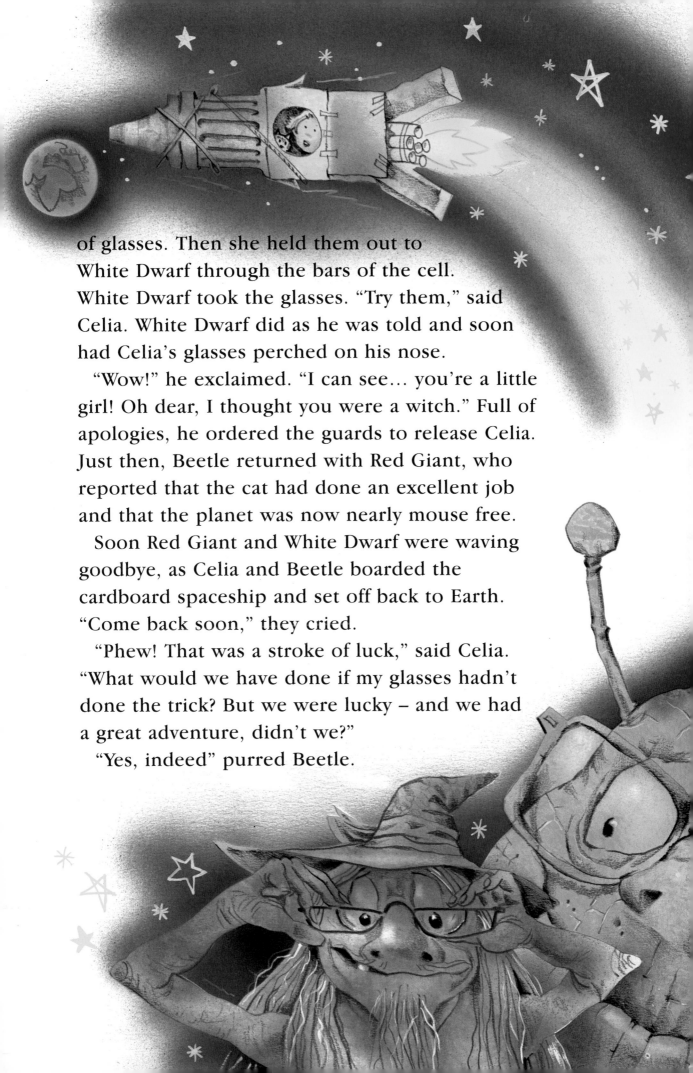

of glasses. Then she held them out to
White Dwarf through the bars of the cell.
White Dwarf took the glasses. "Try them," said
Celia. White Dwarf did as he was told and soon
had Celia's glasses perched on his nose.

"Wow!" he exclaimed. "I can see… you're a little
girl! Oh dear, I thought you were a witch." Full of
apologies, he ordered the guards to release Celia.
Just then, Beetle returned with Red Giant, who
reported that the cat had done an excellent job
and that the planet was now nearly mouse free.

Soon Red Giant and White Dwarf were waving
goodbye, as Celia and Beetle boarded the
cardboard spaceship and set off back to Earth.
"Come back soon," they cried.

"Phew! That was a stroke of luck," said Celia.
"What would we have done if my glasses hadn't
done the trick? But we were lucky – and we had
a great adventure, didn't we?"

"Yes, indeed" purred Beetle.

The Monster No-one Believed In

The monster lay in the mud at the bottom of the lake, thinking. Cold currents of water swept over her. She was sad. Everything had changed. Once, she'd been the most famous monster in the world. People had travelled from far away in the hope of catching a glimpse of her. They had camped beside the lake for months, waiting for her to make an appearance. Books had been written about her, television programmes – even full-length feature films – had been made. There was a visitor centre where people could see photographs, models and videos, and a shop with plastic replicas of her, postcards, T-shirts and key fobs – all for her, the monster in the lake.

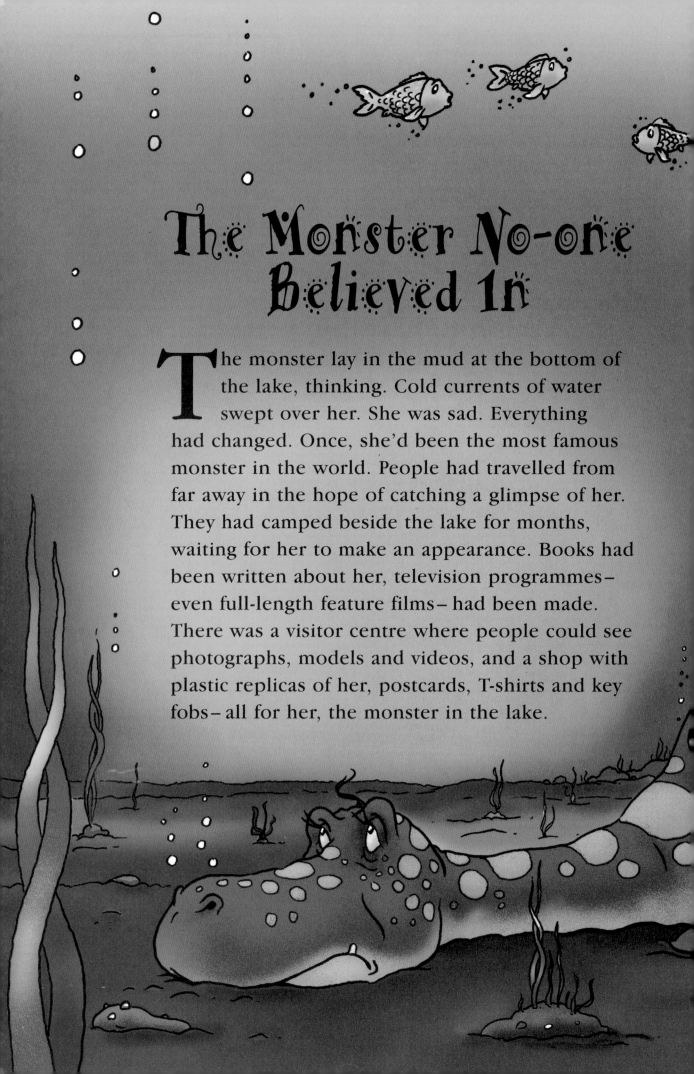

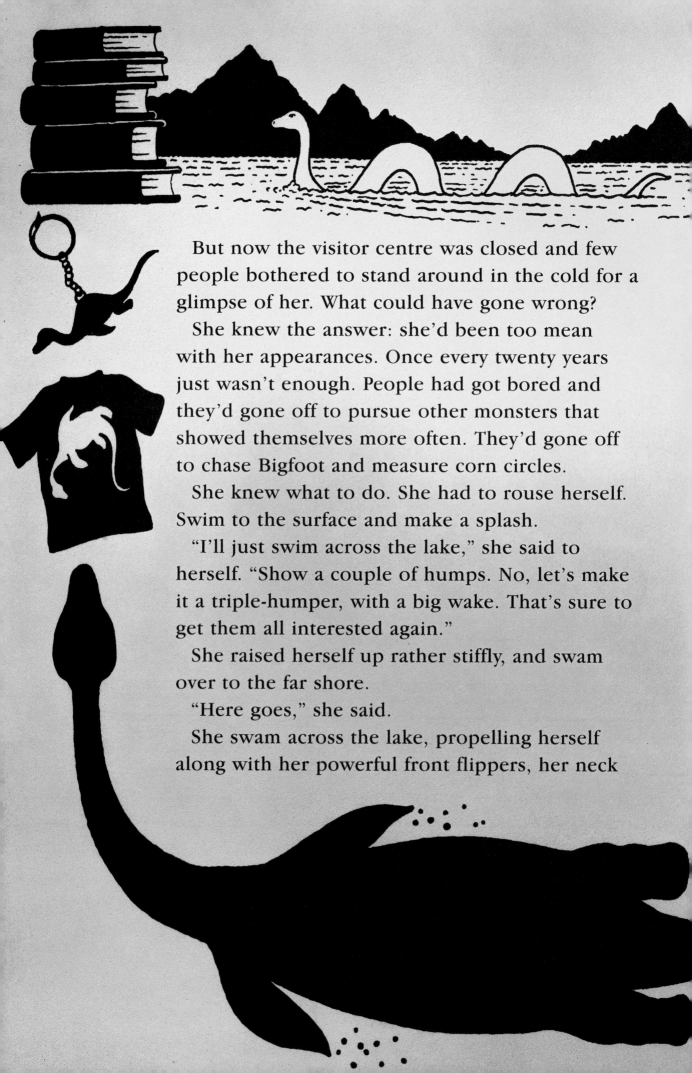

But now the visitor centre was closed and few people bothered to stand around in the cold for a glimpse of her. What could have gone wrong?

She knew the answer: she'd been too mean with her appearances. Once every twenty years just wasn't enough. People had got bored and they'd gone off to pursue other monsters that showed themselves more often. They'd gone off to chase Bigfoot and measure corn circles.

She knew what to do. She had to rouse herself. Swim to the surface and make a splash.

"I'll just swim across the lake," she said to herself. "Show a couple of humps. No, let's make it a triple-humper, with a big wake. That's sure to get them all interested again."

She raised herself up rather stiffly, and swam over to the far shore.

"Here goes," she said.

She swam across the lake, propelling herself along with her powerful front flippers, her neck

outstretched, her legs trailing along behind her
like tree-trunks, her big spotted back breaking the
surface of the water. Nothing could make a wake
like that, not an otter or a floating log or a big fish.
She knew that when the people saw it, there'd
be a frenzy of activity with cameras flashing and
helicopters full of journalists. She'd be all over
the papers the next day.

She lifted her neck out of the water and looked
towards the shore. It was empty. There was no-one
there. In the distance, she could see a campsite
with lots of colourful tents. There were people
there, but they weren't looking towards the lake.
They were sitting outside their tents, reading
newspapers and frying up sausages for supper.
Others were playing football. No-one was
interested in her.

The monster drifted sadly back to the bottom.
It was no good; no-one believed in the monster
in the lake any more.

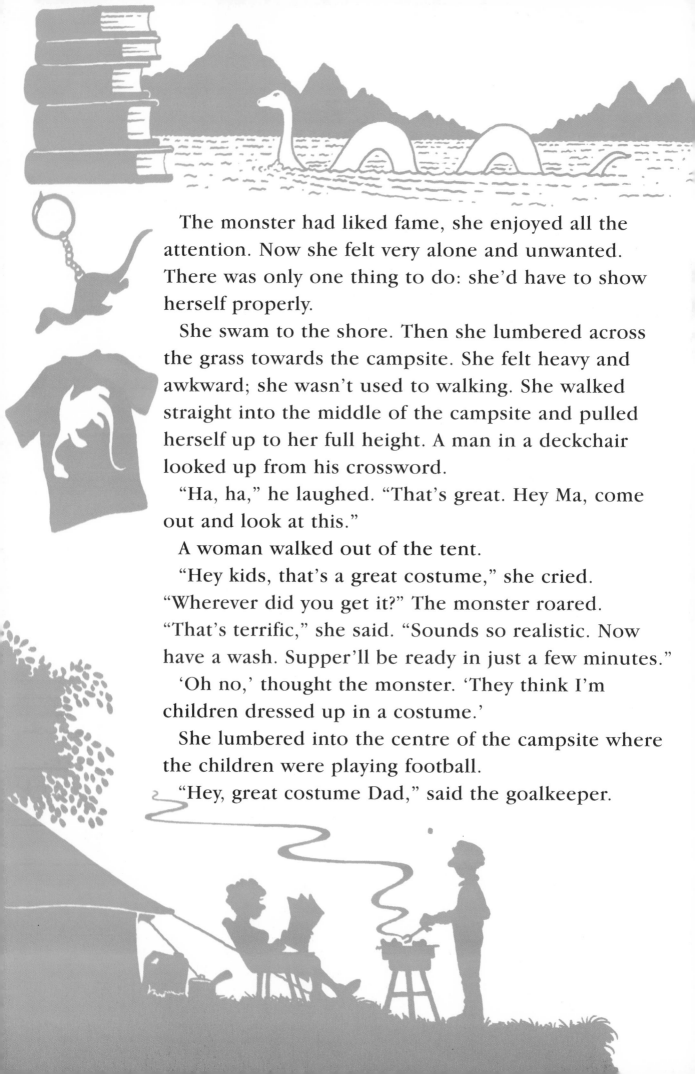

The monster had liked fame, she enjoyed all the attention. Now she felt very alone and unwanted. There was only one thing to do: she'd have to show herself properly.

She swam to the shore. Then she lumbered across the grass towards the campsite. She felt heavy and awkward; she wasn't used to walking. She walked straight into the middle of the campsite and pulled herself up to her full height. A man in a deckchair looked up from his crossword.

"Ha, ha," he laughed. "That's great. Hey Ma, come out and look at this."

A woman walked out of the tent.

"Hey kids, that's a great costume," she cried. "Wherever did you get it?" The monster roared. "That's terrific," she said. "Sounds so realistic. Now have a wash. Supper'll be ready in just a few minutes."

'Oh no,' thought the monster. 'They think I'm children dressed up in a costume.'

She lumbered into the centre of the campsite where the children were playing football.

"Hey, great costume Dad," said the goalkeeper.

"You look just like a monster. But can you get off the pitch? We're in the middle of a game here." The children carried on playing, passing the ball around her and shouting, "Joke's over Dad. You're spoiling the game."

The monster walked sadly back to the lake. She slumped gloomily down by the water's edge, her neck hanging wearily. Just then she heard footsteps. She looked up to see a girl walking quietly along. The girl didn't see the monster until the last moment. But when she did, her eyes became as wide as saucers and she let out a scream.

"It's the monster!" she shrieked.

"Oh, I wouldn't bother yourself with all that," said the monster to the astonished little girl. "Nobody will take any notice."

"Wh-wh-why?" stammered the girl.

The monster explained that no-one believed in her any more – everyone thought she was just someone in a costume.

"My ten thousand years of fame is over," she said sadly. "I suppose it couldn't last forever."

"Well, I believe in you," said the girl. "We'll have to think of something that will get everyone's attention. I know – why don't I drift out onto the lake and pretend to be in trouble. Then you can rescue me. They always make a big fuss over someone who rescues a person. Then they'll see that you're the real monster and you'll make it into the headlines again."

The monster smiled. It was as good a plan as any. She slipped once again into the cold water. The little girl climbed into a boat and rowed herself expertly out onto the lake. Then she deliberately pushed the oars away.

"Help! HELP!" she cried, standing up in the boat and facing the campsite. The campers heard her and came running to the shore.

"Get another boat," cried someone.

"Ring the coastguard or the fire brigade," shouted another.

Just then, right on cue, the monster reared
up out of the water. She hadn't meant it to
be such a dramatic appearance, and she hadn't
meant to be so close to the little girl's boat,
but it was too late now. A great wave engulfed
the boat, tossing the little girl into the water.

"It's the monster," cried a distraught woman,
"and it's attacking my daughter."

"Get a gun," cried someone. "Call the army."

"Oh, no," thought the monster. "That isn't
what I had in mind."

"Help," spluttered the girl.

Reaching down, the monster plucked the
little girl out of the water with her huge jaws.

"It's eating my daughter!" cried the woman.

Slowly, calmly, holding the girl in her mouth,
the monster swam to the shore and put
her down in front of her mother.

The woman was relieved that her

daughter was safe and her cries changed to "The monster's saved my daughter."

Everyone took up the cry. "The monster saved the girl," they cried. "The monster's a hero." Cameras were flashing, video cameras whirred and the monster could hear the steady chop, chop, chop of a helicopter as it approached.

'I think that's enough for me,' she thought. 'I'm off.' She turned gracefully and dived, down to the bottom of her lake, leaving the excited campers on the shore still cheering and shouting and reaching frantically for their cameras and mobile phones.

The monster sank into the mud at the bottom of the lake. 'I think I'll lay low for a while,' she thought. 'Just for another 20 years or so. A monster can only take so much attention, after all.'

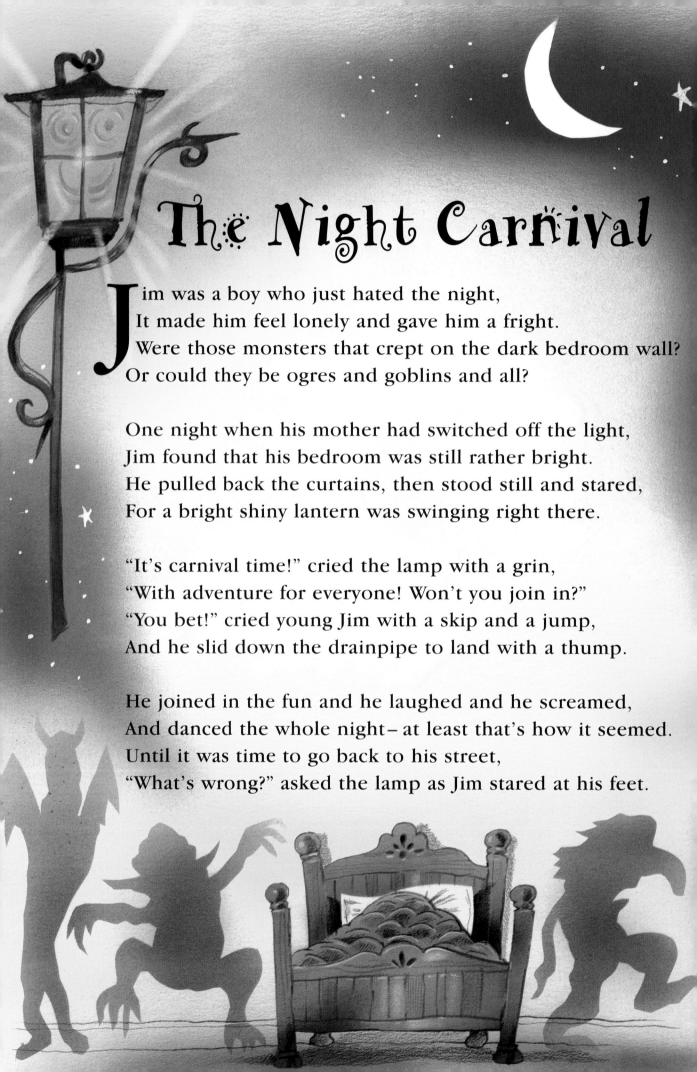

The Night Carnival

Jim was a boy who just hated the night,
It made him feel lonely and gave him a fright.
Were those monsters that crept on the dark bedroom wall?
Or could they be ogres and goblins and all?

One night when his mother had switched off the light,
Jim found that his bedroom was still rather bright.
He pulled back the curtains, then stood still and stared,
For a bright shiny lantern was swinging right there.

"It's carnival time!" cried the lamp with a grin,
"With adventure for everyone! Won't you join in?"
"You bet!" cried young Jim with a skip and a jump,
And he slid down the drainpipe to land with a thump.

He joined in the fun and he laughed and he screamed,
And danced the whole night– at least that's how it seemed.
Until it was time to go back to his street,
"What's wrong?" asked the lamp as Jim stared at his feet.

"I'm scared of the dark," he replied, "Can't you see?
My room's full of monsters. I'm sure you'll agree!"
"They're not monsters at all, Jim!" the lantern replied,
"They're carnival folk– so there's no need to hide!"

"I've got to move on," said the lamp with a sigh,
"Have a peaceful night's sleep, Jim. I'll bid you goodbye!"
Jim's bedroom returned to the darkness once more,
And the shadows and noises were there as before.

But when Jim looked out from behind both his hands,
He didn't see monsters, just carnival bands!
Now Jim is no longer afraid of the dark,
In fact, he now thinks it's a bit of a lark!

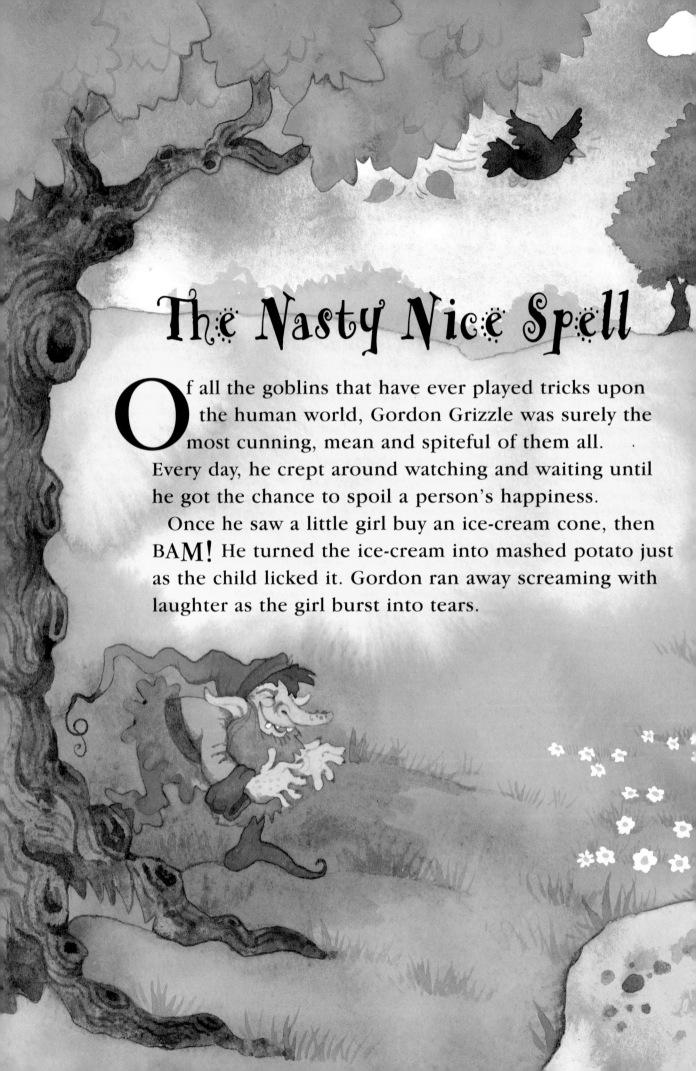

The Nasty Nice Spell

O f all the goblins that have ever played tricks upon
the human world, Gordon Grizzle was surely the
most cunning, mean and spiteful of them all.
Every day, he crept around watching and waiting until
he got the chance to spoil a person's happiness.

Once he saw a little girl buy an ice-cream cone, then
BAM! He turned the ice-cream into mashed potato just
as the child licked it. Gordon ran away screaming with
laughter as the girl burst into tears.

Another time he saw a man arrive at a house holding a bouquet of roses behind his back. The man's sweetheart opened the door, but quick as a flash, Gordon was there. BAM! To his horror, the man presented the woman with a bunch of leeks. Gordon danced with mirth as the woman slammed the door in the young man's face.

Gordon's reputation was so bad that even the other goblins were wary of him.

"That Gordon Grizzle will go too far one day!" warned Marcus Mildew, who was a very wise old goblin. The other goblins nodded their heads and scratched their scruffy beards thoughtfully.

"But what can we do?" Marcus continued, as the other goblins shook their heads sadly. "I'll think of something," said Marcus at last.

The next day, when Gordon was snooping around looking for something really nasty to do, he overheard a conversation between two women.

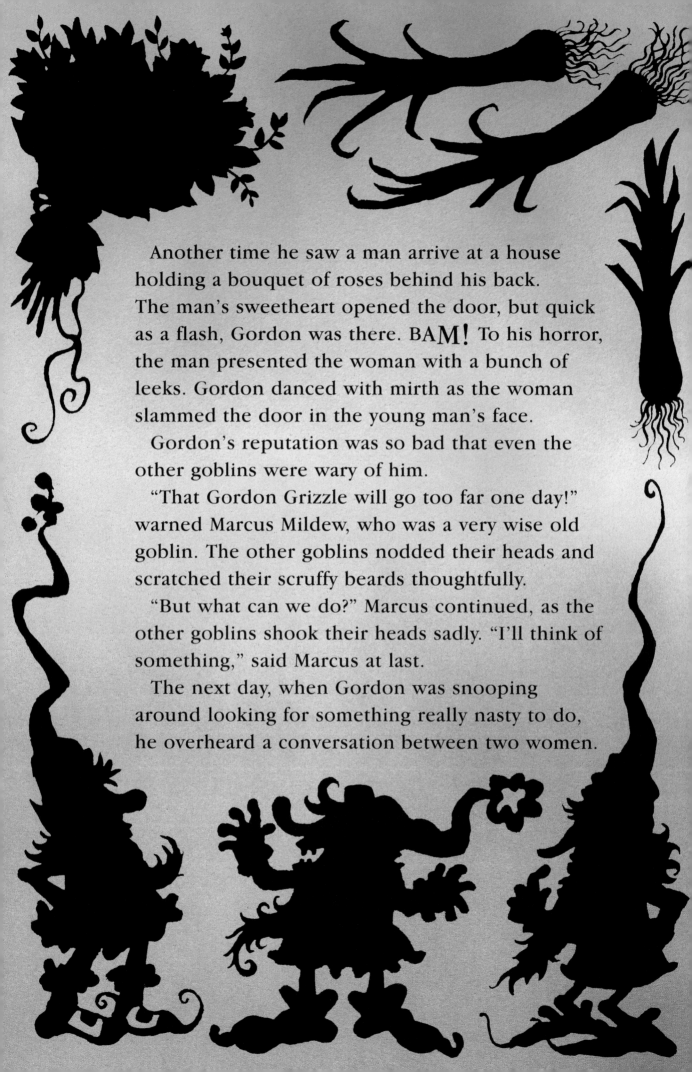

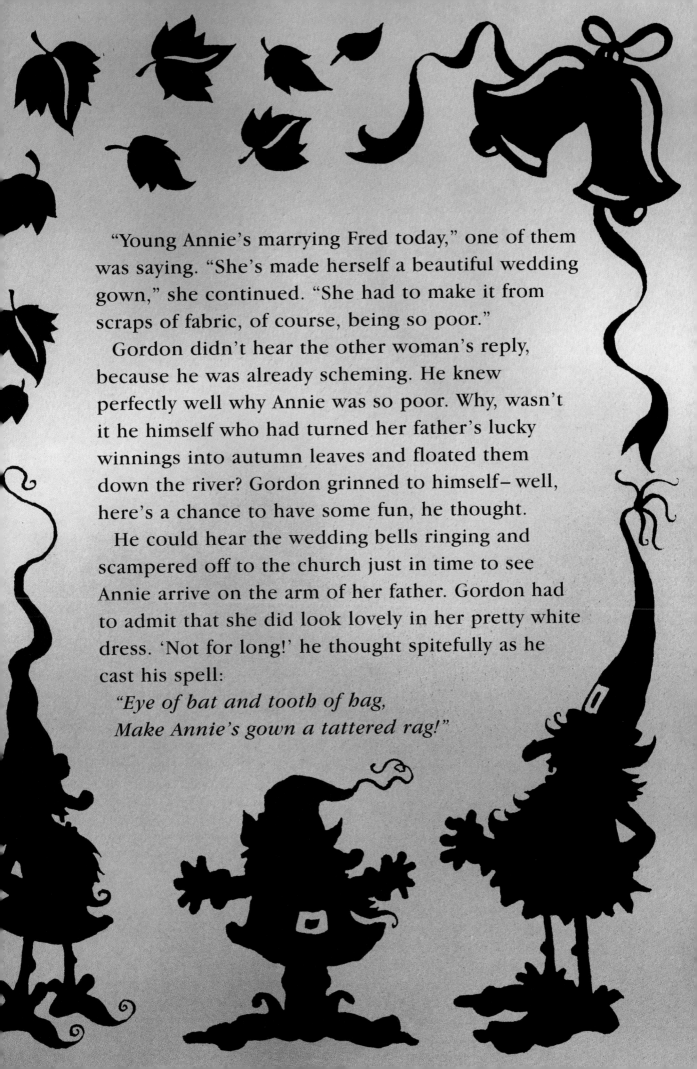

"Young Annie's marrying Fred today," one of them was saying. "She's made herself a beautiful wedding gown," she continued. "She had to make it from scraps of fabric, of course, being so poor."

Gordon didn't hear the other woman's reply, because he was already scheming. He knew perfectly well why Annie was so poor. Why, wasn't it he himself who had turned her father's lucky winnings into autumn leaves and floated them down the river? Gordon grinned to himself– well, here's a chance to have some fun, he thought.

He could hear the wedding bells ringing and scampered off to the church just in time to see Annie arrive on the arm of her father. Gordon had to admit that she did look lovely in her pretty white dress. 'Not for long!' he thought spitefully as he cast his spell:

"Eye of bat and tooth of hag,
Make Annie's gown a tattered rag!"

BAM! The deed was done. Gordon giggled to himself. He didn't even bother to look back as he slipped in through the church door. He heard the wedding guests gasp as they turned to look at Annie. "Ha, ha, ha– I bet she looks truly awful," he sneered. "Now let's see to the groom!"

"Slimy slugs and all things naughty,
Make Fred's face look old and warty!"

BAM! There was another gasp from the people as they turned round to stare at the groom. Annie's jaw dropped in amazement.

Gordon peeped out from behind a pew. To his utter astonishment, there stood Annie in the most gorgeous silver gown that he had ever seen. A beautiful diamond tiara held her veil in place, and Gordon could see her eyes fill with tears as she smiled at Fred.

"Oh, Fred!" she breathed. "You look so… different."

Gordon spun around to look at Fred. He looked not old and warty but younger and more handsome!

What's more, he was impeccably dressed in
a suit of rich velveteen. Gordon was livid.
This wasn't what he had intended to happen!
The young couple looked happier than ever and
that wouldn't do at all. He shook his fists and
stamped his feet with rage. Then he began to
realise something. He was jealous.

"It's not fair," he wailed to himself. "I want to
be happy, too!" Soon he cast another spell:

"Banana skins and custard pies,
Make me happy, healthy, truthful and wise!"

'That's better!' thought Gordon, skipping out
of the church, though he didn't actually feel any
better. In fact, he felt much worse.

'Ah, I know what I forgot!' he thought:

"Dragon's toe and ogre's head,
Make me young and handsome – just like Fred!"

Now, he felt really very peculiar. He seemed to be shrinking and looking down, he saw to his horror that in place of his leather boots was a pair of slimy, green, webbed feet. Gordon realised that he had turned into a toad!

"That'll teach you!" said a familiar voice from high up. It was Marcus Mildew, but Gordon could barely see him over the top of his highly polished shoes.

"I've been watching you, Gordon," said Marcus. "I've seen your spiteful ways, spoiling everyone's fun. So I decided to spoil your fun, too! From now on, every time you cast a bad spell you'll find the opposite happens. And you're going to remain a toad until someone shows you some kindness." And with that, Marcus was gone.

Gordon stared at his long, wet toes. Now he understood why all his spells were going wrong. What had he asked for? To be happy, healthy and wise – and handsome! And now he was the opposite of all of these. Oh dear! He really felt very sorry for himself.

There was no time to dwell upon his misfortunes, however, for the world was now a very dangerous place. A pair of yellow eyes loomed towards him – a cat! Gordon sprang high into the air just as the cat pounced, narrowly missing him with its sharp claws.

'I'm feeling parched. I must get to water,' thought Gordon, though he had no idea which way to turn. The trouble was, being so small, everything looked different. He looked through a sea of legs and feet on the pavement.

'I'm sure there's a stream on the other side of the road,' he thought. Dodging the feet, he hopped his way to the edge of the pavement, and was nearly squashed flat several times. Monstrous cars

roared past and Gordon was too petrified to cross the road. Then he spotted a boy pointing at him.

'I hope he's going to show me kindness,' thought Gordon, quaking with fear. To his horror, though, he saw the boy pick up a stone. The boy raised his arm to hurl the missile and Gordon closed his eyes in fright.

"Stop!" called a voice. Gordon opened his eyes to see Fred scolding the boy. Then he knelt down and gently picked Gordon up. "Let's take this poor toad back to our garden, Annie," said Fred.

Soon Gordon was sitting on a lily leaf in the middle of Fred's pond, watching all the wedding guests having a party. He looked at his reflection in the water – and looked again. He was a goblin again! Without thinking, he dived in and swam to the edge of the pond.

What a sorry sight Gordon was as he crept home with his clothes dripping and stinking, and covered in slimy duckweed. But I think he'd learned his lesson, don't you?

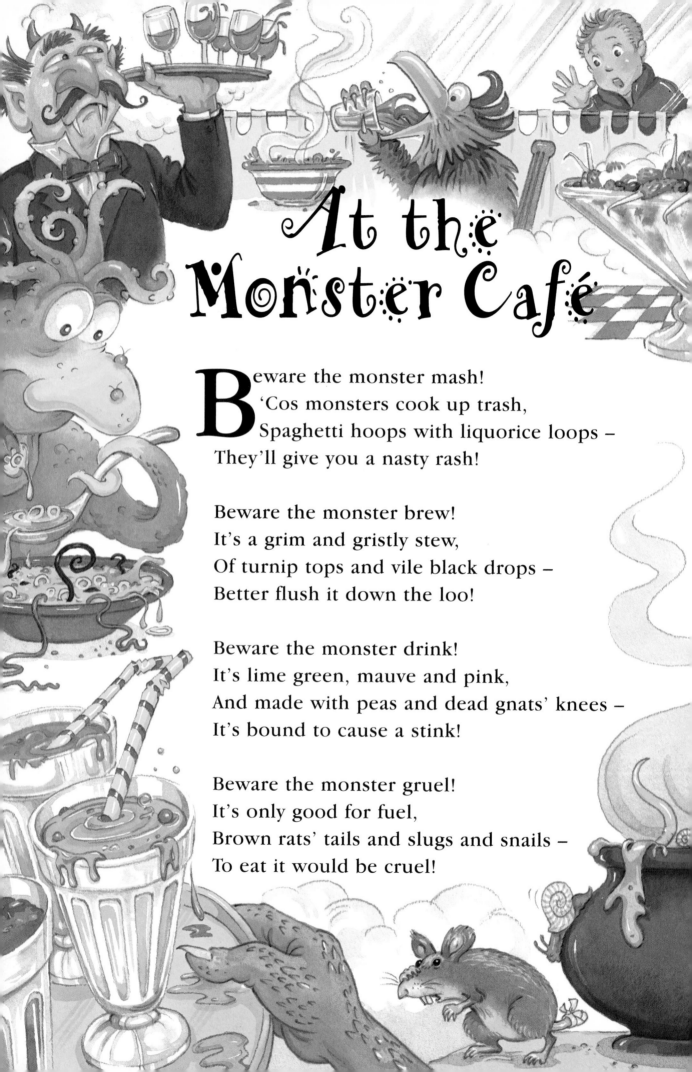

At the Monster Café

B eware the monster mash!
  'Cos monsters cook up trash,
  Spaghetti hoops with liquorice loops –
They'll give you a nasty rash!

Beware the monster brew!
It's a grim and gristly stew,
Of turnip tops and vile black drops –
Better flush it down the loo!

Beware the monster drink!
It's lime green, mauve and pink,
And made with peas and dead gnats' knees –
It's bound to cause a stink!

Beware the monster gruel!
It's only good for fuel,
Brown rats' tails and slugs and snails –
To eat it would be cruel!

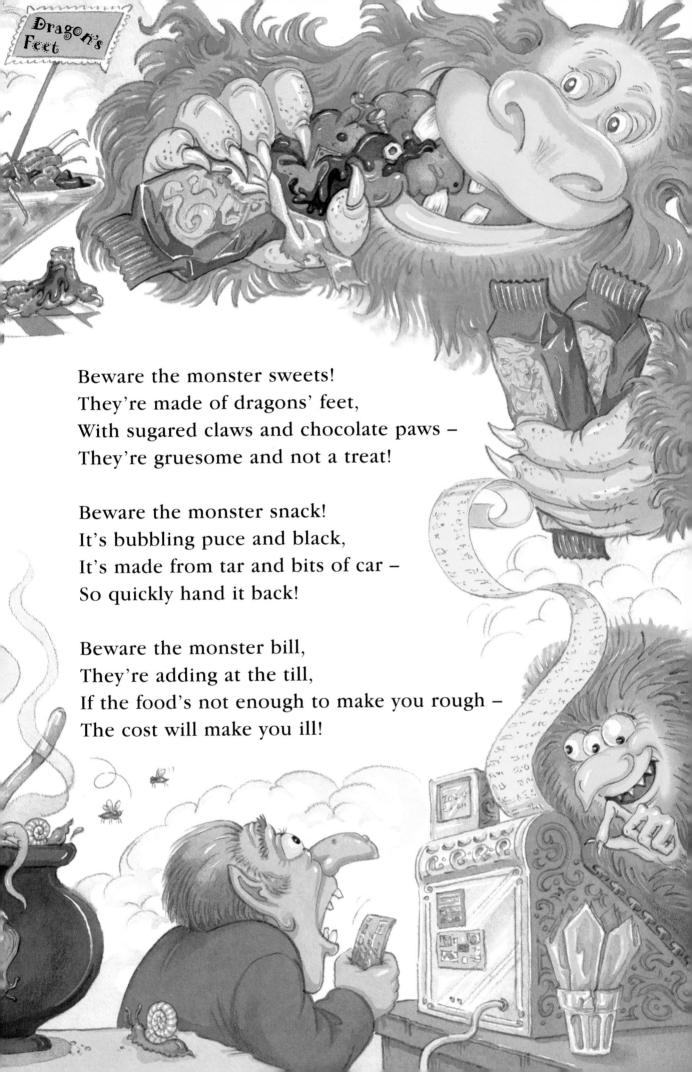

Beware the monster sweets!
They're made of dragons' feet,
With sugared claws and chocolate paws –
They're gruesome and not a treat!

Beware the monster snack!
It's bubbling puce and black,
It's made from tar and bits of car –
So quickly hand it back!

Beware the monster bill,
They're adding at the till,
If the food's not enough to make you rough –
The cost will make you ill!

Why the Sea is Salty

Long, long ago, when the world was very young, the oceans and seas were almost the same as they are today. Their waters were just as blue and just as many waves beat upon the shores – and just as many pebbles were thrown up onto the beaches. But, there was one very big difference. In those far away days, the oceans and seas were not salty. No, not one bit. People would come down to the shore each day and fill their buckets with water to drink. And, in those days, the sea water was cool, clear and sparkling, and it tasted delicious.

Now, at that time there lived two giants named Og and Ig, who were brothers. While Og lived in a large dwelling beside a lake, Ig occupied a tumbledown hut halfway up a mountain. Although they were brothers, the pair of them were as different as the sun is from the moon. Og was strong and fearless. He swaggered about the land, roaring at the top of his voice. If anyone crossed his path, he would uproot a tree with his bare hands and hurl it at the poor, unfortunate person. As he had but a single eye in the middle of his forehead, Og was very short-sighted, so he usually missed his target, but not before he had scared his intended victim witless.

"I am Og the brave!" he bellowed. "No-one will defy me!"

Og's brother Ig was the total opposite. He was gentle and timid, and very frightened of his brother. He had but one leg, so he limped about with the aid of the branch of a tree, which he used as a walking stick.

When Og wasn't out and about terrifying people, he was at home cooking. He had a huge appetite, so every day he would roast a whole ox for himself. Then he would eat a mountain of potatoes and wash it all down with great jugs of beer. His culinary skills were basic to say the least, but he was immensely proud of his cooking and thoroughly enjoyed his huge feasts.

So much so, indeed, that every day he would make a cauldron of his favourite soup. He made the soup according to a recipe that he had found long ago and had memorized. Being short-sighted, unfortunately he had misread the recipe. Where it said "Add a pinch of salt," he had read "Add a packet of salt." So each time Og made the soup, he would add a whole packet of salt!

Did Og care? Not one little bit! He never, ever tasted one drop of his soup. The reason he made it was so that he could invite Ig over for dinner, to make him jealous. Ig was far too frightened of his brother to refuse.

So every evening, Ig would make his way slowly and painfully down the mountainside to Og's house beside the lake. Og would give Ig the cauldron of salty gruel while he tucked into his roasted meat. Now Ig was timid, but he wasn't stupid. He knew perfectly well that Og was oversalting the soup. He also knew that his brother was very short-sighted. So every evening, Ig would pretend to drink the soup.

"Particularly delicious soup!" he would lie, smacking his lips and rubbing his belly. At the end of the meal he would say to Og, "I'm tired brother. I'm going home. I'll take the leftovers home to have tomorrow. Goodnight." Og's mouth was usually too full for him to do more than nod and grunt.

Then Ig would heave the cauldron of soup onto his frail back and make his way slowly and painfully back up the mountainside to his own home. Not once did Og offer to help – which was probably just as well, considering what Ig did to the soup when he got home.

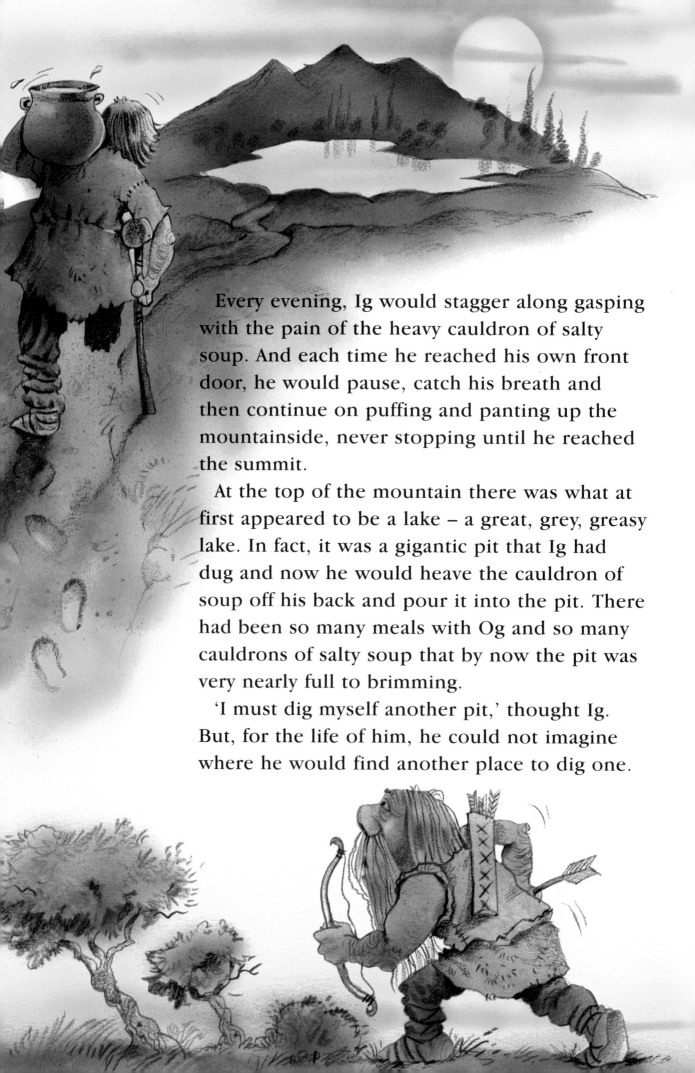

Every evening, Ig would stagger along gasping with the pain of the heavy cauldron of salty soup. And each time he reached his own front door, he would pause, catch his breath and then continue on puffing and panting up the mountainside, never stopping until he reached the summit.

At the top of the mountain there was what at first appeared to be a lake – a great, grey, greasy lake. In fact, it was a gigantic pit that Ig had dug and now he would heave the cauldron of soup off his back and pour it into the pit. There had been so many meals with Og and so many cauldrons of salty soup that by now the pit was very nearly full to brimming.

'I must dig myself another pit,' thought Ig. But, for the life of him, he could not imagine where he would find another place to dig one.

One evening, Ig and Og had their meal together as usual. And, as usual, Og tucked into his roast ox, while poor Ig pretended to eat the ghastly salty soup. It was a lovely evening, and after Ig had left, Og decided to go out for a walk. In spite of his huge dinner, he was still feeling a little peckish, so he took his bow and arrow with him in case he should spot a bird or animal to shoot.

He set off up the mountainside, and after a while he spotted something ahead of him on the path.

'What a strange humped animal!' thought Og. 'I've never seen one like that before. I wonder if it's tasty?'

Of course it was Ig, with the cauldron of soup, ahead of Og, but with his poor eyesight Og could only roughly make out his shape.

Og followed Ig all the way to the top of
the mountain, then he watched as the
'animal' paused and lifted its hump off its
back. Og, who was ready to take aim, was so
astonished that he dropped his bow and
arrow. What happened next amazed him even
more. The animal seemed to pour a great deal
of liquid from the hump, then it turned to
leave the mountain top. Then Og saw its face
and realised it was Ig.

He was about to call his brother's name,
but then he thought, 'I'll find out what he's
up to first.' As soon as Ig had disappeared
down the mountainside, Og rushed to the
summit and peered over. There was a great,
grey, greasy lake! Og sniffed, and then he

sniffed again. "Funny," said Og to himself, "that smell's familiar!" He scratched his big bald head – then he understood…

"My soup!" he roared. "He's been throwing away my soup!" At first he was furious. He stamped his giant foot and flexed his massive muscles. "I'll show him!" he growled. But then, quite unexpectedly, he began to cry. "All these years, he didn't like my lovely soup!" Og wailed.

A big, fat tear rolled out of Og's huge eye and hung for a moment, before falling down, down into the lake. It was too much. As the tear hit the lake, the great, grey, greasy, salty liquid spilt over the brim and rushed down the mountainside in a huge torrent, sweeping all before it.

It lifted Ig's hut clean off the mountain and Og's house too. On and on the torrent roared through woods and valleys, across pasture and meadows until finally it reached the sea. Only then did the salty soup stop. It mingled with the water of the oceans and the seas, and to this day, you will find that the sea is salty.

As for Ig and Og, they clung to each other as the torrent of salty soup rushed past them. They watched in horror as their homes were swept away. When all was calm again, they continued to hug each other. It was the first time in all their lives that they had embraced.

"I think we need each other, don't we?" said Og. "With my bad eyesight, I can't build a new home on my own."

"And with only one leg, I can't either," agreed Ig.

So the brothers built a home together and lived there for the rest of their lives. And every evening, they both sat down to a wonderful feast, and Og never served salty soup, ever again.

The Perfect Couple

(to the tune of *Here Comes the Bride*)

Here comes the bride,
Big, fat, and wide,
Nice rotten teeth, in a
Smile filled with pride.

Huge goggly eyes,
Great wobbly thighs,
Long matted hair and the
Scent of pigsties.

Here comes the groom,
Fresh from his tomb,
Shuffling along with a
Look full of gloom.

Skin grey and dank,
Hair long and lank,
A face that is crumbling and
Stench rather rank.

Oh, what a pair,
Folk stop and stare,
Brave ones take photos – but
Just for a dare!

So, you may weep,
Your flesh may creep,
But it just proves
Beauty's only skin deep!